Men Hurt

Men Hurt

Jasmine Herring

Copyright

ISBN-13: 978-0-9909919-5-3

ISBN10: 0990991954

The Butterfly Typeface Publishing
PO BOX 56193
Little Rock Arkansas 72215
www.butterflytypeface.com
butterflytypeface.imw@gmail.com

Dedication

To my Uncle "Ruffy" William, the most influential male role model in my life. In the absence of my father, you've stood in and been such a great support. I thank you for your love, your guidance, and your infectious personality. With love always, your niece!

Everyone tells me that I should say goodbye

But all I want to do is ask you why

Did you think about the tears you left behind

Or did you only have yourself in mind

I'll never know if you ever loved me

For that part will forever be a mystery

Because of where you are now

I have to find a way to make it, some way some how

Contents

CHAPTER ONE

No One Understands

"Just look at him over there," said Mary Ann.

"As handsome as can be and with a college degree. I wish they made men like him for my age. Michelle and Leroy must be very proud."

Watching from afar as my nephew mingled around the living room, thanking all who came out for his open house, "Yes they are. We are all proud of the fine young man he has become."

Excited for my nephew's future endeavors, I could not help, but to feel sorry that more of his friends weren't as fortunate in life. "It's a shame that more of his friends are not here to share in the same success."

Shaking my head in devastation, "Many of them have turned to the streets either selling or on drugs, others locked behind bars, and the rest," taking a deep breath as I was well acquainted with many of his former friends, "deceased."

Making eye contact with my nephew who glanced over in our direction, I could not dwell on the path many of his friends decided to travel for this was not a day to mourn, but a day to celebrate all that had been accomplished by my nephew, Chris. Now a college graduate, no criminal record, having yet to be classified a baby daddy as this generation lacked proper etiquette, single, and prepared to take the world by storm, "I just thank God that my nephew made it to graduation having not been influenced by the streets, never once calling a jail cell his home, or viewing his lifeless body in a casket. Just look at him. This here is a priceless moment for the entire community."

Tears of joy formed in the corners of my eye sockets as I continued to stare in amazement. I watched this young man form in each stage of life, aiding his parents in the upbringing of a young prince with a few whoopings along the way, a firm believer that it takes a village to raise a child. Looking at him in such a positive light, I was truly honored to be called his Aunt.

My sister, who could not be still even if for two seconds to socialize, was headed in the direction the ladies and I had made our gathering corner. With a tray of cupcakes in one hand, a bowl of chips in the other, and a pack of unopened napkins dangling from her teeth, our dear friend sparked a conversation with a touch to her hand as she attempted to whisk by, giving only a wink. Assisting with the items she currently possessed, "Michelle, you and Leroy must be very proud of Chris. He is such a fine young man."

Remaining in constant motion, Michelle, following every direction the tray, released from her hand went, responded in a rushed tone, practically begging to exit our circle and return to her duties as the host, "Yes we are."

Forming her lips to release a tiny ounce of air that appeared to create an overwhelming amount of emotion, it was at this moment that Michelle finally let go of all that was hindering her from getting close to the guests in her home.

It was obvious that she was keeping busy and remaining distant as a way to block the feelings inside that all parents face when their children reach milestones in their lives. Knowing my sister, the feelings she bottled inside could not hide for long and were bound to be exposed, one way or another. Sitting down with the ladies and myself, finally, we bared witness to a mother who was extremely excited and saddened all at the same time.

Making her focal point her son, who stood in laughter with his guests, delivering a long-winded breath, accompanied by a short-lived display of laughter, she said, "Our baby boy is all grown up."

Each of us consoling Michelle who had begun to cry, some rubbing her back while others extended a hand of support, the girls were curious as to the next chapter of her son's life.

"So what are his plans now that he is finished with his undergrad," asked Dona.

Angling her head towards the sound of Dona's voice, with a response of sarcasm, Michelle replied, "He has this silly idea of relocating to New York which I don't believe is a good idea."

Looking at the group of ladies, hoping to gain the support of someone who also found the idea of traveling to New York as silly as she, "I told him that he should wait and save his money before exposing himself to such a big city. He has worked so hard and I mean, my husband and I just want him to be fully prepared for the adult world and all that comes with being on his own."

No sooner than Michelle finished voicing her concern did we hear a familiar voice surround our circle, instantly posing a question to my sister, "Haven't you already prepared me mother," said my dear nephew himself, the subject of conversation. Putting on his charm as only he could, "How are you beautiful ladies doing this afternoon?"

Attempting to change the conversation, stepping in as his favorite auntie, I lightened up the mood, hoping to soften the subject and get back to congratulating the man of the hour, "Hey baby boy? What's new with you?"

Plopping down on the couch next to his mother, placing his palm on her knee, staring directly into his mother's eyes, "Oh nothing, just enjoying this lovely party that mom dukes and dad put together."

The circle, enjoying Chris's company, that is until Messy Kathy had to open up her big mouth with her untimely, stir of the pot comment.

Revisiting the New York conversation as if she did not get the vibe that the topic was fragile, Kathy asked, "Your mom told us you're thinking of taking off to New York. Is that true?"

No, she just made it up Kathy, I wanted to say out loud. She always knew how to add fuel to the fire which is why I held my head low as this was the only way to keep from delivering an unfiltered response on behalf of my sister whose eyes cut like a knife.

"Oh, did she," asked Chris.

Exuding a look that appeared to be some code only he and his mother were aware, like that of an annoyed appearance as I know Michelle had made her attempts to steer him from New York, Chris walked right into the door that had just reopened.

In a confident tone, Chris set the record straight as it pertained to his future, with a firm, "YES."

He proudly announced, "I will be leaving in two weeks."

Talking with his hands, allowing them to guide his words, "I am waiting on the office to confirm my move in date. I have a couple of interviews lined up as well so, Lord willing, New York will be my new home." It appeared that both Michelle and Chris were on two different pages about his future which explained further, Michelle's emotions. Here we all believed that he was only pondering a trip to New York when in fact, he was dead set on residing in New York.

Dona, directing a question to Chris, with a voice of concern, asked, "Considering that you just graduated, are you sure that you are not rushing this move honey?"

Her limits reached, everyone talking over her, Michelle intervened, hearing no one else out, clearing her name and setting the record straight, once and for all. Looking deep into her son's eyes, she said, "In no way am I attempting to discourage you son. I just don't want you to go down to such a large city unprepared and with your eyes closed shut."

Placing her palm on top of his which remained on her knee, all had a front row seat to both a passionate mother and son who undeniably loved one another, but held different views neither eye could see. Michelle, attempting to prove her case, "Dad and I have no problem with you staying here while you get yourself together. You've already accomplished so much and for that, we are very proud."

Chris, returning the hand gesture his mom had just released, placing the opposite hand on top of hers, "Mom, if I do not go now, I'll never know what it's like to truly be a man. It's bad enough that I let you talk me into staying home instead of on campus during my undergrad."

Breaking the skin to skin contact, Chris removed his hand from his mothers, extending his palm in the air, signaling that he did not want her to take offense to his respectful rebuttal, "Don't get me wrong; I certainly appreciate all that you and dad have done, but I did not experience living on my own because I stayed home upon your request."

His hand now planted firmly on his chest, "I have to do this for me. You and dad have been around to teach me many life lessons and they won't go away just because I relocate to another city. You have to trust in the decision that I am making for my life."

Chris, making many valid points and pleading his case, had the entire circle on his side. My sister had lost the war. Her baby boy was now a man and clearly held a great head on his shoulders. We did not know what Michelle was preparing to say next, but whatever it was, it was not going to change the made-up mind of my nephew. Words ceased from all parties, I took the floor saying not what my sister wanted to hear, but what needed to be addressed, "I hate to say it Michelle, but it sounds as if his mind is already made up."

Standing behind my big sister, rubbing her shoulders to comfort and also pin her down in case she felt the urge to stand and become violent towards me, "He has a good head on his shoulders. Hearing his well-spoken, thought out plan, he knows what he's doing. If he is going to make errors in life, he is going to have to learn to fix them on his own. We can only cover our children for so long and pray that the morals and values we've set for them, are not forgotten and that God leads them when they stray."

As I assumed, my words were interpreted as an attack, causing my sister to swiftly turn towards me. Firmly rubbing her shoulders, in my mind I was keeping her still and in her seat as she released her anger, using me as a scapegoat, "You have no idea how I feel. I love my son. This is my one and only child. I just don't want him to do anything that he is going to regret and for that, I will not apologize as his mother and protector."

Kneeling down at the knee level of his mother, Chris pleaded, hoping to bring some peace to his mother's worry, "Then show me by accepting my desire to move away to better my career. Besides, I cannot stay away from you chocolate drops for long," winking at the ladies that surrounded both he and his mother.

Resting his head on his mother's knees, "You know I love you boo."

Finally, laughter filled the circle and most importantly, a smile was displayed on Michelle's face as only he could trigger.

A subtle slap to the back of his head she released,

"Chris, get out of here. That smooth talk isn't going to work forever."

Laughing in a sneaky manner, "It did get me through twenty-two years now. You know what I'm saying?" A lighter vibe surrounding the group now that it seemed Chris and my sister were on the same page. Returning our thoughts to the excitement and congratulating of my nephew, each of us exchanged words of encouragement as the proud graduate prepared for the next chapter in his life.

"We're proud of you Hun," I said as his aunt.

"The sky is the limit Chris," said Mary Ann.

Dona, close family friend, "Remember, trust God sweetheart. He'll lead and guide you."

Thanking all who offered well wishes, Chris politely excused himself from the circle as more of his friends entered through the front door. His exit allowed for Michelle and I to hash out our tit for tat with one another. She always attacked me for taking everyone's side, but hers, which was never the case. Anyone that knew me, understood that I never sided with anyone simply because of a bond that we shared. I spoke truth whether you wanted to hear it or not which should be no surprise to my sister after all this time.

"Listen Michelle," I voiced.

The circle minimizing as some bid their goodbyes while others headed out onto the patio for a bite to eat, "I know exactly how it feels to watch your children leave the nest. When Austin Jr. and Alexis moved away, I was devastated. Everyone reached out to me the same way that I am reaching out to you today. I heard, but did not listen to all of the advice the outside world thought that they were giving me.

My children not coming home every day, having no one, but my husband and myself to make dinner for, fewer loads of laundry to wash, and the overall laughter children bring, now gone, was no easy pill to swallow."

Walking over to the punch bowl as I became parched having spoken so much, Michelle and I reconvened our sister to sister talk in the kitchen over a glass of lemonade, "There were days where I wanted to break down and cry."

Laughing at how silly I behaved during the time my children went away, "I recall sitting in their rooms just waiting for them to show. Sometimes I would reach out by phone just to hear their sound on voicemail. But one day," and I had to lean in for this one as I did not want anyone else to depict a mental image of my husband and I, "Big Austin came out into our living room "naked" and my life forever changed."

Michelle, practically spitting out the lemonade she had not yet swallowed, "After that night, he and I began doing things around the house that we could never imagine doing with the kids home. Trust me, fear of the unknown is hard, letting go, even harder, but your intimate life is about to sky rocket like," not knowing how loud I had gotten, getting a bit hot and bothered thinking of my husband, "WOOOO," I expressed, patting the sweat from my forehead.

Those near, startled at the level of my shout, myself having to contain my own volume, I placed my back to the crowd whose attention I had just captured while laughing with my sister.

"You are leaving too many pictures in my head nasty," Michelle responded with a smirk.

Making amends with a hug to end the conversation, my sister went back to her duties as the host of Chris's open house, but not before telling me that she appreciated our talk, "You are crazy girl, but I hear what you're saying."

CHAPTER TWO

Not A Little Boy Anymore

As my open house concluded, I did what any appreciative child would do and began picking up around the house to assist my parents. My mother remained in the kitchen, quieter than usual which meant that she had something that she wanted to get off her chest, in her own time that is.

"Mom and Dad, the party was incredible. It was good to see the family together again." My father, breaking down the tables in the living room, waved his hand at me and said, "I'm glad you enjoyed yourself son."

My mother, releasing a delicate smile, had yet to utter one word, prompting me to further my gratitude, "I appreciate everything you guys have done for me." Placing the trash bag down that I had used to collect waste around the house, I sat on the bar stool next to the kitchen counter, reminiscing on the past four years in college.

"When Mike passed away, my soul was crushed. I no longer wanted to go to college knowing that he would not be by my side. If it wasn't for you mom and you dad, I don't think I would have had it in me to even finish, let alone hold a degree in my hand today." Dad coming to my aid, knowing how sensitive of a subject Mike was, came forward and placed his arm around me, "What happened to Mike hurt us all son, but there was no way in hell that I was going to allow you to use his death as a crutch for not going to college."

Resting an arm on my back, with the other, dad flagged

mom over who was dedicated to scrubbing the only dish that remained in the sink. "Michelle. You agree with me, right?"

Collecting myself, I too stared at mom and asked, "You've been quiet for a while now mom. Is everything ok?" Turning off the kitchen sink, fanning her hands in the air to dry off the water, mom finally joined in conversation, standing idle by the counter, "I'm ok son."

Hopping up on the bar stool closest to me, using her hands to aid her words, "I'm just trying to wrap my mind around the thought of you leaving. You haven't even found a job yet and New York is very expensive. How do you plan to pay for this condo and various living expenses?" Pulling my phone from my right hip, I opened up the Chase app just to show mom and dad, mostly my mother, just how responsible I truly was as she still found me incapable of making it on my own, "I do have a savings account. I've been putting money aside from my work study since sophomore year of college. You and dad did teach me how to plan, prepare, and budget remember?"

Mom, holding possession of my phone, scrolled with a fine-toothed comb, examining each and every deposit that I'd made, leading up to the current balance remaining today. Nothing to hide, wanting her to truly feel relieved, I allowed her all the time and access that she needed to my account. Not a single word, I tapped her knee, wondering what else she could possibly think to say, "You thought you raised a knucklehead, didn't you? I will be fine just trust me."

Laying my phone face down, turning as our knees aligned with one another, "I trust you son; it's others that I am not so trusting of."

Dad, easily irritated, put this back and forth conversation to rest, standing in between my mother and myself.

Staring directly at my mother, "Leave the boy alone already Michelle." My mother, frowning at dad, was the champion for having the last word. Disregarding dad's plea to let me be, "Chris, you are my one and only baby and you have to understand that this is not easy for me to process. You have been a part of my life for the past twenty-two years and I love you more than I ever thought I could love a person." Taking slight offense, dad questioned my mother's love for him as she made my dad appear nonexistent, focusing on me alone, "Hello over hear. You do love your husband, right?"

Giving dad the hand, "Leroy hush. Do you really have to ask if I love you fool?" Shrugging his shoulders, "You completely left me out of the equation of those you love."

"I'm having a moment with my son if you don't mind," her eyes doing a complete three sixty turn. "I've been married to you for the last eighteen years. Is that not punishment enough," mom smirked, laughing in a sinister manner just to get a rise out of dad. Standing from her chair, placing her hand on my shoulder, "A mother's love for her child is hard to describe. Chris, I know that you will go off and do great things, I'm just going to miss you. That is all son."

Mom, joining alongside dad, I gathered the feeling that she was slowly accepting the fact that there was no changing my mind about New York. Hearing her out, I gained a better understanding of where her heart was. She wasn't in doubt that I could not survive on my own, she just had a hard time expressing the fact that she was going to miss me and as much as I tried to hide it, I was going to miss her too.

"If you love him honey, you have to let him go," Dad said. "Chris is not the baby boy you keep referring, but a grown man that we have raised to love and respect. He has been brought up with the ability to decipher right from wrong."

Taking a seat, my mother, no longer standing side by side dad and I, left the two of us, Dad's hand firmly placed on my shoulder as he attempted to summarize mom's thoughts, "What your mother is trying to say son is although we will both miss you, we want you to follow your heart's desire." My neck turned at mom, extending my hand in hopes that she would latch on, "Is that true mom? Do I have your blessing to go?"

I could tell that she had to reach from the core of her vocal chords to deliver, not the response she wanted, but the one she knew she had to. This response, which separated me from the boy she brought up to the man that I became, "Yes son. I support your decision." It was hard for my mother to give her blessing as I prepared to depart to New York. Watching her shed a tear was even harder to swallow making me second guess if in fact, I was making the right decision. I too, was scared to embark on a new journey as I had never been away from my parents for more than a few short days.

They were always there to pick up the pieces of my life, but this new chapter was one I would need to experience alone. It wasn't enough to just state that I had a degree, but applying that degree and moving forward with my life, now that was a sure sign of success which I yearned for. A life that would not allow mommy and daddy to run towards every mistake I could possibly make. "Come here mom and dad," bringing us together in a huddle form. I extended my arms out to embrace them both with a hug filled with an abundance of love. This moment, I would treasure forever as I believe it symbolized twenty-two years of togetherness. Taking a mental snapshot to hold still this very image, all that I would have to hold on to as I prepared to travel the road that lied ahead.

Road Ahead

"Do you think you have enough socks and underwear," mom asked while sitting on my bed, refolding all that I continued to throw into my suitcase. Dad, giving me space, lending his support out in the hallway, had heard enough of mom directing and double checking all that I was doing. Frustrated to the max, he spoke in a loud tone, "Michelle, I am sure that whatever Chris does not have, he will be able to purchase at any surrounding store from here to New York. Let the boy go already."

Scratching his head, dad left the hallway near my room, stomping his feet down the stairs, painfully annoyed by my mother's behavior. Sympathizing with mom, dad's delivery a bit harsh, I welcomed her help despite how upset it made my father.

"Mom, I'm fine, but thank you very much!" Here I was attempting to get dad off mom's back who then handed me a twelve gallon fully stocked cooler, "I made you some meals so you won't have to stop while on the road."

A few meals, now that was an understatement as I glanced in the cooler. Shaking my head at the fact that mom had prepared everything from sandwiches, juice boxes, chips, carrot sticks, as if I were walking into my first day of kindergarten. Siding with dad as I was capable of picking up anything else I may need, including food while on the road, I wanted to decline the offer of such a plethora of food. Out of respect, I accepted the gesture and listened as she rationalized her actions, "The last thing I want you to do is find yourself hungry, having no choice, but to eat at a hole in the wall restaurant with a million health code violations.

The next we'll get a call that you've been admitted to a hospital with food poisoning before you even make it to New York." I couldn't help, but to laugh at my mother as she had the most serious look on her face, explaining all that could happen to me if I did not accept her food. Holding the cooler with both hands awaiting myself to take ownership, "This should last you through the duration of your trip."

Dad, able to hear as mom secretly attempted to smuggle food my way, made his voice known from all the way downstairs, hoping to hit my mother right in the eardrum, "MICHELLE. STOP IT AND LET THE BOY GO. DAMN."

Eyes rolling in the back of her head, not the least bit concerned with what dad had to say, "SHUT UP LEROY. If you don't like what I am saying, don't listen." Taking one final walk thru of the room I spent my infant, adolescent, and teenage years, I closed the door for the final time, mom standing directly alongside me as she'd always been; right by my side. Hand in hand, together, we walked down the stairs step by step, meeting dad at the bottom of the staircase just waiting to put an end to mom's coddling behavior as he saw it. Intervening the side by side position mother and I currently stood, he pushed me forward, breaking the interlocking of fingers between mother and I and with a voice of seriousness along with a stare and eye roll to mother, said to her indirectly, "Come on son, I'll walk you out."

Dad, not making this departure easy on mom, forced me to ignore his urge to step outside, that is until I said goodbye to mom first. I wanted her to know that I was not at all cosigning any of dad's behaviors and that I was going to miss her. It was because of her that I was taking this leap of faith. Her love, her guidance, her constant prayer, shaped who I was and for all of these reasons, I was forever grateful. Guided out of the front door by dad's forceful touch, I planted my feet firmly to the ground, dad trying his best to keep mom away from me.

Just barely holding my balance, dad using all of his might to push me forward, I turned around once more and kissed the forehead of the most important, influential woman in my life, "I love you Mom and I don't know where I would be without you!"

Thinking my parting gesture of a forehead kiss would invite my mother to follow father and I to the car, instead, she pushed away at my chest, face buried in her palms, and walked into the house hiding an overflow of tears that seeped through the separation of her fingers. I contemplated running in after her, not wanting to leave on such a somber note. My feet firm and still, I glanced over at dad and knew that I did not have to chase after mom for she was in good hands. Even though he had a hell of a way of expressing his love and care, dad would be there to comfort and/or annoy which would distract her long enough to think I was gone on a mini vacation and not an extended stay.

For this reason, I did not see any point in following behind. The only child, I knew where the emotion was coming from and could not blame her. Dad on the other hand, was always the stern parent. He did not believe or partake in the overly nurturing mannerisms mom delivered on my behalf and never strayed from practicing and preaching, "spare the rod, spoil the child," as mom did.

Assisting as I loaded my luggage into the trunk of the car, questioning any further items I may have left in the house, "Is this everything son?" Eyebrows up, both index finger and thumb surrounding my chin, I quickly rewound the tape on all if any items I may or may not have left behind. "Yes sir. I believe that's all."

Standing on my left, wrapping his arm around me for the second time; his hands heavier than bricks, dad took one look back towards the house, guiding me a few steps forward, close to the end of the driveway.

Staring behind us yet again, he handed me a package with great care and with mysterious affect, "I did not want to give you this in front of your mother, Lord knows how nosey she would have been."

Out of nowhere, dad began impersonating mom, carefully glancing over his shoulder, not wanting to admit that no matter how tough he appeared to the eye, deep down we all knew mom wore the pants. Standing before me, pointing his finger in the air, "Leroy what's in that box?"

With a high octave tone, one in which could be heard from the vocals of a woman, my mother to be exact, he imitated further, "Let me see that box. I thought you told me not to baby him. Look at you being a hypocrite." Laughing hysterically together as he played her to a T, one turning the corner to our street could capture a genuine moment shared between father and son which unlike most of my friends, I could recall numerous occasions such as this. Both of us secretly taking in this final bonding moment, quiet and still, dad stepped in, speaking softly for the first time ever, "Open this once you get settled in New York and give me a call once you have."

Left alone with the mysterious box that came with verbal instruction, I watched as dad turned his back and walked in the direction of what would now be considered my former address.

"What is it dad," I couldn't help, but ask.

Curious as to why he wanted me to wait hours before opening the box when I could do so now and thank him in the moment, he repeated a direct order, "Boy just do as I said and be careful out there." You could always tell when my father was trying to hide and contain his emotions, emotions he vaguely displayed. His exit was always smooth and at the end of the sentence which he tried hard to rush, his voice would always break into a high pitch.

Even if he did not verbally state that he loved or would miss me, I knew that he did as I had grown fond of reading his behaviors, "I will dad." Watching my father part ways, it hit me, I was the man that I was today partly because of him as well. This man, proud to call my dad, stepped in as such a powerful force and example in my life, one I prayed to have similarities. No words suitable enough to express my appreciation for having my dad in my life, I shouted whatever came to mind hoping to catch him before he walked inside the house.

"HEY DAD."

Stopping, his back still turned, I ran to meet him, the gravel under my feet making my presence known, "Did you forget something son?"

Face to face we stood, our eyes in direct contact of one another, I sensed that he may have just recently shed a tear or two, explaining why his back was turned for a period of time, "No, but I almost did." Confusion written all over his face, my sudden leap back towards the house not yet explained.

"I just wanted to say thank you! Thank you for teaching me how to be a responsible man. So many of my friends lacked proper role models growing up, but I always had you. Sometimes I was jealous that you took some of the guys under your wing because you were my daddy, not theirs. You were always the neighborhood father that everyone gravitated towards. I loved so much that you were my actual father. Every lesson you have taught me, I will use to make you proud of me." Unable to fight back the emotions, dad's eyes turned red in color and from each socket, an overflow of tears released, tears he couldn't hide even if he tried.

His voice cracking, coughing, trying to play off his visible tears, "I am already proud of you Chris!" I brought it in one final time before I headed back to my car. Placing one arm around the others shoulder using the second to pat away at the back, I held on to this feeling, one I did not want to let go.

This was my number one guy.

I would paint the city red over this man here. I swore to myself that I would not get emotional saying goodbye to my mother and father, but here I was five minutes alone in the car, my mother and father inside the house, and still, I remained in the driveway looking back and forth from the front windshield to the rearview mirror.

Was I making the right decision to move fourteen hours away? Through my front windshield, I captured a glimpse of my mother stating, "Don't go son."

Looking at the rearview mirror, an unknown destiny was displayed. No further hesitation, I placed the car in reverse, kissed my front windshield, and headed towards the highway, passing the old stomping grounds on the way. From the basketball court the boys and I would play twenty-one, some games more serious than others to the McDonald's on the corner of Valley Road where we would put our change together and buy a super-size drink to share causing a scene when one of us backwashed. These were memories that I would take with me and hold dear to my heart.

Turning right onto the highway, it was official; I was leaving my roots to sew new seeds.

CHAPTER FOUR

Home Sweet Home

Two hours on the road and I found myself having to search for new radio stations as the few select I had become accustomed and set on my cars radio player, had since lost signal. Failed attempts to find new tunes I could groove to, I turned to both the passenger and back seat of the car to start a conversation. Hearing the echo of my voice only, it dawned on me, I was alone on a vacant road.

It hadn't yet settled that my parents were not coming with me on this journey, one in which I would have to travel on my very own. Missing them already, not used to the distance, I reached for my phone resting on the front seat, attached to the charger and debated on calling them to keep me company.

Playing hot potato with my phone while keeping my eyes on the road, I began contemplating this call I initially needed for comfort. Not only would this sudden communication paint a picture that I was possibly second guessing the decision to leave, but could very well startle my mother as I'd only been gone a few short hours. Putting my quest to rest, I eliminated the thought to contact my parents, taking in the scenery as a remedy for the loneliness within.

Alone on the road, I allowed myself to consume each and every piece of food mom had tightly packed in the cooler; food that was to last fourteen hours. Hungry again, I had to make a decision, one in which my mother wouldn't be too pleased.

Against my mother's wishes, the restaurant exit sign calling my name, I took the next right just off the highway and swore a vow of secrecy between myself and my stomach. The two of us had an agreed upon understanding to never, ever tell my mother that I stopped for food, especially in a town I had no prior knowledge existed. She was always worried about the food I consumed out of her sight, who cooked it, as well as the ingredients contained. In her eye, if she was not the hand that prepared the food, it was deemed hazardous.

With one car parked behind the building, two additional in the front, I became a bit skeptical about this establishment. The longer I contemplated, still a passenger in my car, the louder my stomach roared, forcing me to tuck away my fears and send a quick prayer above over the one cook they had inside of the restaurant who also took and served the orders.

Good Eatz was the name of the restaurant and either the name was an indicator that the food was in fact good or it was meant to lure patrons into the building, walking out, filled with regret. Examining my surroundings, I found one customer sipping what appeared to be a cup of coffee as they blew and carefully took small sips at a time while the other, one booth in front of me, continued to poke at what appeared to be some form of cobbler or pie that had not yet sparked their taste buds. Taking a deep breath, I carefully extended my arm out onto the table I occupied and courageously searched up and down the two-sided, laminated menu. Coincidentally, just as I flagged down the waiter slash cook slash server, my phone began to ring. It was none other than my mother who had impeccable timing.

Staring at the screen on my phone, waiting to see if she were going to leave a voicemail, it seemed my phone was never going to stop ringing. Afraid to answer, it wouldn't take much for mom to get the truth of my whereabouts out no matter how hard I tried to keep silent.

She was the queen of third degree and never backed down. Glancing down at my watch which rest upon the table I had been gone a few hours now which she had probably held off as long as she could not to call and so I decided to answer, putting her worries to rest. Making sure to mute the call upon conclusion of each sentence I spoke, this effort in attempts to eliminate any background diner noise, "Hello." Following my very own cue card, I placed my phone on mute.

"Hey Chris, mom was just checking on you. Where are you?"

Taking the phone off of mute, speaking quickly as the waiter slash cook slash server was heading in my direction and could blow my cover, "Uh......... I'm just parked at a rest area. I needed to stretch a bit before getting back on the road."

Extending my arms into the air as I really did have to stretch, I completely spaced putting the phone back on mute.

"Sir, would you like a refill," the waiter slash cook slash service asked. My cover was blown, and I wasn't sure how I was going to get out of this one.

"A refill? Chris where are you," mom's voice high pitched with a stern twist. Quick on my toes, I responded, "I told you mom, I'm at a rest area. That was an ad on the radio."

How convenient of her to call in the middle of ordering food from the very place she requested I not go. I began to wonder if she had placed a tracking devise somewhere on my body, calling at the exact moment I was preparing to eat someone else's food other than hers.

"Well ok son. I was just making sure that the drive was going well. You remember, if you get tired, pull over and rest. You cannot start a career, dead. Be careful and cautious of others. Do you hear me?"

My mother was always far reaching in conversation. Here I was heading to New York and death just so happened to be what was on her mind. That was my mother for you.

Laughing, tickled by her conversation, "Yes mom, I hear you. I love you." Tickled as well, she released a brief giggle, "I love you too son. Goodbye."

It was never my practice to lie to my mother especially over something so small, but I knew that if I told her my exact location, I would be given the third degree which was an all-night, worthy of pulling over conversation that I just did not want to have.

I'm telling you, people were really sleeping on these hole in the wall type restaurants, including myself. Surprisingly, the food was actually pretty good. I could only imagine how many tourists passed by just because of the outside appearance. If I ever found myself back this way, I would certainly return.

After paying my bill, tipping the waiter slash cook slash server who proved great at multi- tasking, it was time to head back on the road and accept what my future had to offer.

Punctuality was a trait I possessed and wasn't about to stray simply because I was out on my own and without constant reminders from my parents. Unless I found myself with car trouble or in need of gas, any further pit stops would have to be postponed as I was on a strict schedule.

NEW YORK

Welcome to New York City, the sign read.

I had made it in one piece and entirely on my own. This was honestly one of my first solo accomplishments without the aid of my mother and father. As much as I wanted to call them in excitement as if I were a small child having received an A+ on a test, I stood firm, now a man on my own, and backed down from the urge. In my mind, I knew they would both be very proud and didn't need any verbal recognition.

After crossing New York lines, I contacted the realtor to inform him that I had made it in town and still planned to meet at our scheduled appointment. I then programmed the exact address of my new condo on my dashboards navigation. Lord knows I'd be lost had I not had my GPS system. One thing mom was right about which took me only a short time to agree; New York City was popping. I mean, cars were bumper to bumper in traffic, if you commuted by foot, you were shoulder to shoulder with the person walking next to you and there was hardly enough room for the cyclist to join on the busy streets.

Thirty minutes of driving, I was less than 100 feet from the garage of my condo and I could hardly contain myself. It was surreal stating, "MY CONDO." I had never owned property in my life and now, I was walking into my first home. This ownership allowed for so many freedoms I would not have had sharing a home with both my mother and father. I could turn up all night playing my music as loud as I wanted, entertain a few guests without questioning whether or not mom approved, drink out of the jug without dad sneaking up behind me and slapping me in the head, I could even wake up in the morning and walk out into my living room butt naked and do you know what; THIS WAS MY HOUSE.

I would not have to hear my mother rant, "Turn that down. Christopher tell your friends it's time to go home. Boy, stop drinking out the jug and get a damn glass," or my all-time favorite, "Chris why are you bringing these ungodly women into my house?"

This was my palace and I was the king of this here castle.

I two stepped into the elevator, up to the tenth floor where my condo was located. A short distance down the hall stood the realtor as I was let off the elevator and even his presence still could not decrease my vibe. In fact, seeing him only enhanced the turn up so much so, with a little coaching, I had him doing the *dougie* as well. His skills weren't half bad for a white guy.

With the keys in his hand, a pumped-up attitude, John, the realtor asked, "You ready to do this man?" Spending no time contemplating like I had done in my parents' driveway, I punched to the left and to the right like Mike Tyson and said, "Let's do it!" I could hear the metal lock release from its latch in which it was bound. Watching as the door slowly opened before my eyes, a bright light reflecting directly at my chest, so powerful, as if it were welcoming me into my home with such a warm first impression.

John standing still, allowing me a moment to process the overwhelming chemistry I experienced, knowing this was my first place. With a few things left to accomplish before the condo was officially mine, John moved forward with our list of things to do, "Chris. On behalf of the team, we would like to welcome you to New York City. Let's take a final walk through to make sure that you do not have any other questions or concerns."

My condo was better than I remembered. You know when you watch a movie for the second or third time and say, hey, I don't remember seeing that. Those were my sentiments with each room I came in contact, checking for damage or items of poor taste which I found none. Everything was perfect; fresh paint, updated appliances, four bedrooms, a beautiful patio view of the city, along with a much-appreciated care package that sat on my marble kitchen counters. Returning to the kitchen, both John and myself, it was time to seal the deal, "I just need one final signature from you and you are all set my friend." Mom would have yelled at me as fast as I signed the papers, "Boy, don't you dare sign those papers without reading first." But when I say everything was perfect, it really was. What could go wrong?

Putting into the hands of my realtor, John, a signed copy of my new lease, in exchange, he delivered copies to me as well.

Preparing to leave the kings palace, John walked towards my front door offering one final hand, "Is there anything else I can do for you Mr. Harris?"

This condo was all that I could dream. What else could I possibly require of John? Nothing coming to mind, I said, "I think I'm good John. I appreciate your urgency finding me a place as fast as you did. You could not have told me that employers were going to contact me as fast as they had with job leads. You were a god send man."

My hand outstretched, thanking John once more for all of his help, he said, "Don't thank me. This is what I do. If you have any further questions, I left my business cards on the counter. Call me anytime Chris."

Wow! All I could do was stand in amazement. I was the proud occupant of a four bedroom, two-bathroom condo in New York City. Although it was just myself for the time being, I couldn't pass up the price on this particular building. God was definitely in my corner on this one.

With all the extra room in the house, I wasn't sure how to go about filling the space. The thought came across my mind to place an ad online for a roommate, but this was an act I could never tell my mother for she would be on the first flight out. Once I was completely settled in, I was going to determine what to do with three vacant rooms.

My adrenaline still pumping, I began grabbing boxes and bags from my car before all energy was lost. Reintroduced to the box of mystery dad asked me to wait to open, I guided it carefully up the stairs in the palm of my right hand along with my first round of luggage.

"Do not open until you arrive in New York," directed by my father. I examined the box close wondering what was so sacred that my mother was unaware? The suspense taking over, I began to peel the tape off the corners of the box, unfolding one corner at a time and the cat was out of the bag.

It made perfect sense why dad did not want mom apart of such a gift, a gift she'd lose her mind over. Like a jack in the box springing out after the final turn, so too did a rainfall of Trojan condoms. Mom would have fallen to her grave had she been made aware that this was father's parting gift to me, her son, whom she still thought a virgin. There were just certain things I could discuss with my dad that I could not with my mother and sex was one I refused to make a topic of discussion with her.

I was raised in a Christian home and to my mother, sex before marriage was unheard of. Although my father participated in the development of my spiritual upbringing, he was more lenient towards religion as he saw it.

As I began boxing up the loose articles of my parting gift while laughing inside, I noticed a white envelope hidden underneath the plethora of condoms. Inside, I found a receipt for six months paid rent along with a personal note that appeared to be dad's hand writing, "have fun, be safe, live a little, and don't tell mom."

My father may not have been great with words, but his actions always demonstrated his love for my mother and I. As grateful as I was and as much as I appreciated the financial assistance, my concern was whether or not this financial surprise, would set him and mom back on their own bills. I wanted my departure to be a help and not a hindrance making this the perfect opportunity to first, call and let them know that I had arrived to put their minds at ease and second, speak with dad on a personal level.

"Chris? Is that you baby," attempting to play it off as if she did not have the phone glued to her finger tips just waiting for me to call.

Not one to call my mother out, I played it off like I wasn't on to her, "Yeah Mom it's me. I just wanted to let you and dad know that I made it safely."

"That's good to hear son. What do you think of your condo so far?"

Removing my ear from the phone temporarily to take in my new place yet again, I responded with certainty, "I love it mom. You and dad are definitely going to have to come out and visit me. I have four bedrooms. Can you believe it?"

Neither mom or dad had seen the place as this was a personal choice I had made for myself. Sure, four bedrooms was a bit much, but had you seen the price, you would have jumped at the offer too.

Knowing mom; however, it did not matter what kind of deal I received; she would find problems where they did not exist.

"What do you need with four bedrooms," her screeching voice excitedly yelled. "You better not occupy those rooms with women. Don't be bringing any babies into this world without finding you a good Christian woman."

Anytime the word "women" was mentioned, a conversation was bound to ensue. It was more of me listening and my mother babbling.

"Now Chris, I know that having a new place may stimulate the urge of sexual temptation, but remember son, you are a respectful man and I want you to do right by a singular woman. Don't use your new house as a bachelor pad. Find you a church home in the city and meet a nice Christian woman; not some fast tale gal that your generation I believe calls, a THOT. Did I use the right word?"

Did this woman really just use the word THOT? "Mom you are silly."

Putting her mind at ease, I was not currently in the market for a girlfriend, wife, or family. Yes, I eventually wanted to settle down, but in a new city and on the hunt for employment, this was the least of my concern.

"Don't worry mom, your son needs a job before he finds a woman and I promise, she will not be a THOT as you put it." Feeling that she and I were on the same page, "That's good to hear," mom confidently responded.

"When it's time to settle down, I promise, I will do it the right way."

Placing all concern and worry to rest with mom, I still had words to exchange with dad before getting some shut eye, "Is dad nearby mom? I need to holler at him for a moment."

For the first time, mom did not attempt to continue on with conversation as she shouted for dad who appeared to be in another room, "Leroy, your son is on the phone."

Pushing the box side to side on the kitchen counter, I wasn't sure whether to start by saying thank you or asking about the rather large payment.

"What's up son?"

Double checking that mom was nowhere around, I asked, "Is mom close by?"

Dad, sounding a bit confused, "You just talked to her. Want me to grab her again?"

Not at all wanting dad to get mom for the conversation would lead all the way into the next morning, "No. I just know that she often lingers on the phone and did not want her to hear the conversation or get you in trouble."

"In trouble? Why would I find myself in trouble with

your mother?"

Focusing on the box again, holding it up to the phone, forgetting that dad wasn't granted the ability of x-ray vision, I enlightened him, "The large deposit dad. I'm extremely appreciative, but I feel like that may have set you and mom back and if that's the case, I want you to take it back."

Dad clearing his throat, "Like you son, we too have extra money that we don't tell you about. I wanted to make sure that you had some time to get your finances in order. I understand wanting to be independent and I trust that you would not place yourself in a position of strain, but I knew that you would not tell us whether or not you needed help so I thought this would find you relief. Also, because I know that you will eventually have sex, I wanted peace of mind knowing that you were protected."

So focused on the money, it took dad reminding me of the condoms given as well; another example of dads love for me, his son. He may not have been good at verbalizing his love for me, but his actions always proved.

If he said that they were ok, then I had to accept his word for it and move forward, "Dad, this means a lot. Thank you!"

Feeling an emotional moment coming as I could hear dad overcome by the case of the sniffles, he quickly sped up the next sentence in effort to end the call for the night, "You're welcome son now go kill those interviews and let us know when you get the job."

After getting off of the phone with my parents, I walked each room of my home and looked at the emptiness that to a person with a family, could easily occupy, but a person such as myself, not yet a family man, I would be lying if I didn't admit to something missing in my life.

The independent feeling was great, but I had no one to share in this experience or talk to other than my parents. All I had to keep me company were boxes retrieved from the car to unpack, condoms from my father, and a bottle of champagne from the realtor. I guess the only fair thing to do was crack open the champagne, pouring a single glass, and guiding it and myself on to the patio as the sun began to set.

While relaxing and taking in such a beautiful view, I revisited the conversation my mother and I discussed about settling down. Carefully leaning on the balcony, I began to evaluate my life. It was not that I did not want a relationship, but at this moment, I did not believe that I had enough to offer. My dad set the bar high as a man and if I wanted to be anything like him, I couldn't go searching for a queen at this point. To go searching for a mate at this point in life, I feel as though I would ask too much of her financially. I didn't want my queen to lift a finger. I was to be the provider and if a child was created in the process, the struggle would be too great.

Fresh out of college with no job was not the ideal man for any woman and I would never want to introduce myself as such. Women would be around until the end of time and once I was well established, I would go on a quest for Mrs. Right; whoever she may be.

In order to find her, first I had to find a job which is why I called it a night. A broke man was not exactly appealing to the eye and if I didn't call it a night, I was either going to be in the unemployment line or back with my parents.

Prayers up, eyes closed, until morning.

CHAPTER FIVE

What God Has for Me

I'd tossed and turned all night long in my condo, a new surrounding I wasn't quite accustomed. The fear of being late and missing the opportunity to interview with potential employers, had me wide awake and on my toes. I'd even beaten the rise of the alarm clock that continued to sound through the speaker of my phone. Instead of waking me up, it instead, enhanced my excitement to conquer this day.

It was game time and I was ready. I prayed that God would lead and guide me along the way as I made myself known in a new city. A bit nervous, I knew that what God had for me would be just for me, so I shook off my jitters with a little shoulder shake dance and started on my way.

A prayer to start my morning off right as I had practiced since birth, I asked the Lord to show me the plan he had for me and if not either job, to grant within, patience and understanding.

After my morning devotion, I hopped in the shower and searched the box labeled, professional wear in order to find something fitting for the occasion. Beating myself up for not hanging any of the articles of clothing I packed, I was thankful for the restless night which afforded me enough time to get myself together or shall I say, have mom hook me up. I needed a touch from her and fast.

"Mom, would you iron my slacks for me please," shouting from my room, hoping that she could hear my plea.

With no response, I shouted again, "MOM."

Wondering why she had not yet answered my cry, I stepped into the hallway in search of my go to lady. My search, empty, it hit me; I was no longer in the comfort of my parents' house, but in my new home, thousands of miles away from any assistance I was used to receiving.

The task of ironing would have to come from myself and as embarrassing as it may sound, I had never ironed a day in my life which is why I was leaning on a prayer to complete this task. In my head I thought, it wouldn't hurt to give mom a call for guidance. I mean, she did iron my clothes for twenty-two years, but then I thought, I left to gain independence. I had to do this on my own and if I messed up, I'd learn what not to do for the next go around.

First, plugging the iron in, I noticed a dial toward the front and without the aid of a direction booklet, I had no idea what number to set. Deciding to go with the middle number, I prayed that I would not burn my shirt nor pants. After a couple of up and down strokes to my clothes, I took a glance at my work, and I must say, I was impressed. I didn't need mom after all.

A cup of coffee relaxed in my system, giving an added bonus of energy, I reached for my resume which rest on my kitchen island and out the door I walked towards my destiny.

In search of my car entering through the parking garage, I stumbled upon a piece of paper that at first, I thought to leave as it laid on the ground. Unable to get it off the sole of my Stacey Adams, I leaned on the trunk of my car, giving myself that extra balance to remove the debris from under me.

How ironic; I was in search of a church to call home here in the city and under my foot I found a flyer which read, join us for our family and friends day celebration. Not sure if this was God's way of introducing me to this particular church, I was not going to take a chance missing a blessing from him ignoring a possible sign. With my phone, I took a photo of the address as the paper was beyond salvageable to hold on to, carrying with me a visual in case I planned to attend Sunday service.

Having recently spoken to my mother about church, this was sure to bring joy to her ears as I was heading in the right direction and taking with me, many practices handed down by my mother, one being entering into the house of the Lord each Sunday, God willing.

Spending a significant amount of time focusing on the flyer in the parking garage, I needed to head to my first interview before I missed my one and only opportunity with this company.

This was my time to shine and I hoped to move the employers with not only my credentials, but also the many character traits I possessed. As a psychology major, I was blessed with the ability to read others. I felt that with this gift, I would be able to tell whether or not I was of interest to the eye. If they were not impressed I would have to switch my interview tactics to get them to a state of comfortability with who I was and all that I would offer if given the opportunity.

My dream profession was to work with inner city children who struggled with troubled backgrounds. My credibility questioned by some as to how I could possibly relate to troubled children seeing that I grew up in a two-parent household, my response; I witnessed many unstable homes, some having two parents while others had one, if any, who actually remained active in the lives of their children. I was exposed to more than I chose to tell my parents for if they knew all that I had seen as an adolescent, they would not have allowed any further contact with certain friends of mine.

My goal in this line of work was to give these children hope and inspire them to become all that they could despite any trials they may be facing. Both potential employers would allow the opportunity for me to make a difference and I knew that God would reveal to me, the one that he saw fit.

Key in the ignition, head held high, I exited the parking garage claiming a victory.

New York traffic was serious and if you did not allow additional time for your travels, you were bound to be late even if traveling a short distance. It was obvious, those persons running behind for they had this persona about them, as if they were the only ones on the road, disregarding traffic signs. Not a single traffic light, stop sign, or pedestrian walking along the crosswalk was adhered to. I had no problem allowing those privileged motorists full access on the road to cut in front of me for I was not going to start my morning off having been a part of an accident or the newest body count in the cemetery.

My GPS prompting me to turn right in two hundred feet, butterflies began to flutter throughout my stomach as I pulled into the entrance of interview number one. Sitting in the parking lot, I adjusted my rearview mirror, took a good look and patted myself on the back for making it this far. If I did not get the job, the fact that I took a chance coming out to New York, all alone to pursue my career, was worth the applaud. If this was what God had for me, I would walk out the newest member of the team and if not, he had another plan that I was going to wait on.

Binder in hand which contained my resume, I reached in the glove compartment for my binaca, opened wide for two squirts, placed my phone on silent and opened the driver side door, moments away from a verdict. One foot in front of the other, I followed the arrow signs throughout the parking lot which directed me to the front door of the office building.

Hand gripping the front door handle, I walked inside and immediately felt God's presence throughout the hallway. It was almost as if he were standing right beside me holding my hand, telling me that this was the place I belonged.

The gentleman that I was, I took it upon myself to open the lines of communication with the receptionist who appeared just as cheerful as I, the two of us separated by a sliding glass window. Fixing my lips to introduce myself, I leaned on the guidance of my father who taught me to always speak with clear diction and respect. With this bit of advice, I spoke proud and clear, "Good morning! My name is Christopher Harris and I have an interview with Ms. Justine Thomas."

A clipboard in hand, she scrolled up and down with her eyes, responding, "Yes Mr. Harris, I see here that you are scheduled at nine a.m. for an interview. Justine has not made it in yet, but you are more than welcome to take a seat in the lobby and I will let her know that you are here once she arrives."

Looking at my watch, I was pretty early. Day two in New York, I had not yet gotten the traffic down and wanted to make certain that I was on time even if that meant being early, another trait learned by my father.

Preparing to sit in the vacant chair in the lobby, the receptionist whose name badge read, Lori, came out from behind the glass window and offered a suggestion while I waited on Ms. Thomas, "Hey Chris."

"Yes ma'am," I said, eyes forward.

With a smirk, Lori responded, "Chris, you know you don't have to call me ma'am. We're close in age." Most women I knew were so taken off guard at my genuine display of respect. I didn't care if you were younger, older, or the exact age for that matter, I was brought up to respect all women which I expressed, "You deserve respect as a woman and that's all I know how to give."

Without further dialogue, we found ourselves at a standstill. I wasn't sure if my response had offended Lori which could ruin my opportunity for this particular job. Redirecting the conversation, for some reason, Lori had exited the office which I inquired, "Did you need something?"

A light bulb moment shined bright on her face, Lori responded, "Oh yes. If you'd like, while you wait, you can walk around the building and tour the facility. Here's a pass to get through the access doors." Exchanging the access card into my hand, Lori returned to the office where she closed the door, slid the glass door open and called my attention once more.

"Hey Chris."

Politely responding, "Yes."

With a smile on her face, a sincere Lori said, "Thank you for respecting me as a woman and I wish you luck with your interview!"

Nodding my head forward, just before parting ways, "Thank you and you're welcome!"

From an outsider looking in, as I began my own personal tour, it was obvious that the building was in need of some serious rehab. The floor boards were coming up, making it easy for anyone, including myself, to trip and fall. There were leaks dripping from the ceiling tiles, turning certain sections of the once white walls, brown. Just around the corner from the men's restroom, I stumbled upon the gymnasium. Before my eyes, I noticed one young man with serious talent on the court. His hook shot was just as good if not better than one seen by an NBA player. My curiosity intrigued, I stepped further into the gym where I continued to watch, keeping my appearance discreet. This young man played like there was no tomorrow and the longer I watched, I could tell that he was battling something internal, the expression written all over his face.

This being my first encounter with this young man, wanting not to judge, it was apparent that there was a financial struggle in the home. Each time he leaped from the ground to make a shot, his shoes split clear apart forcing him to stop playing and retie his shoe, tighter than the previous attempt. His shirt was also filled with holes and these were not self-created like many kids were designing these days.

His heart and soul put into each move he made on the court, you could tell this was his safe haven, which he felt it best to release his worry. Drawn to this young man, I wanted so much to come forward and introduce myself, offering an ear if need be. No affiliation to the facility just yet, I stayed within my boundary.

"Christopher Harris please report to the front office. Christopher Harris, to the front," sounded through the speaker in the gym. It had been a long time since my name had been called over the intercom. The memories of my mischievous days definitely came to the light listening to Lori state my name.

Quietly exiting the gym, wanting not to disturb the young man, I vowed that if I did get the job, I'd make it a priority to get to know this talented individual.

Down the hall I traveled, in route of the receptionist desk. An unfamiliar face, one I was not yet acquainted, stood, waiting by the office door as I approached. Not a single expression on her face, I could only assume that Lori may have gotten into her ear about my form of respect. Had my interview ended before it even began, I was soon to find out if in fact this was Justine.

Toe to toe, I reached my hand out, introducing myself for the second time. "Good morning. My name is Christopher Harris."

Disregarding my hand and arm which grew tired, the woman, yet to introduce herself, turned to face Lori where they both paused. Laughter shared between the two as if I were not present, I grew further confused.

Her eyes refocused, she extended her hand which reached for my now limp arm, pleasantly responding, "It is nice to meet you Christopher. I hear that you are quite the charmer. My name is Justine and I will be conducting your interview. Follow me please."

Now I knew this was Justine. Trailing behind as she directed me into her office, I watched as Lori continued to giggle, almost running into the back of Justine.

Thirty minutes into the interview, Justine holding for dear life a straight face, I began to feel a sense of defeat as though I did not get the job. Not wanting to waste her time or mine, I put a stop to Justine's drill sergeant question and answer session, "With all due respect Ms. Justine, I get the feeling that you do not consider me a good candidate for the position and I do not want to waste your time if that is the case."

Leaning back in her seat, twirling a pen in between her fingers, she paused, the room still and silent, leaving me trapped inside with the most frightening eye stare.

I'd given my best throughout this interview and had already formulated some ideas for the facility. Prepared to walk out, my head still high, for some reason this woman just would not let me leave which made me wonder if she and Lori were plotting something especially the way that she was giggling while Justine and I walked into her office.

Standing tall and proud, I thanked Justine for her time who then ordered, "Have a seat," as though she were my mother.

I couldn't recall ever obeying a direct order from any woman other than my mother. With great hesitation, I slowly repositioned myself in the chair across from Justine. Lifting forward, resting her hands on the desk, Justine released a smile, the first I'd seen since I met her.

"What makes you think I do not like you," she asked.

Was this woman serious? How about the fact that she avoided shaking my hand upon first contact? How about the fact that she continued to laugh back and forth with her receptionist Lori as if I didn't exist. How about the blank stare that remained throughout the entire interview? She was nice-looking and all, but that stink of an expression on her face made her the least bit attractive and quite frankly, I felt that she was now wasting my time. Clear across town was my second interview, and here I stood in the principal's office, held hostage.

Resume in my hand, which she had yet to ask for, I spoke frank, "If I may, you have held the same blank stare since we sat down. You do not at all seem impressed with the responses I'm giving you."

Out of nowhere, she began to burst into laughter. Either this woman was bipolar or outright crazy. One minute she was frowning and the next, overcome with laughter.

Taking a deep breath, collecting herself from a moment of insanity, "Chris. I watch all of my potential candidates break a sweat. Upon contrary belief, I do like you and would love for you to join our team. That is, if I didn't scare you off."

I didn't know whether to jump in excitement or run out of fear. In the back of my mind I wondered if my boss was truly crazy or if this was in fact, just an act.

A second interview scheduled, I began to think of the young man I had come in contact in the gym. I also thought of the many repairs I noticed around the facility that could use some funding and I started to believe that this was the job God was steering me. The financial burden lifted if I accepted the position, it took all of a few short seconds for me to accept the position. Containing my composure until I exited the building, I thought to immediately contact my mother to let her know that she could worry even less now that I found a job. Looking over my life, I felt so accomplished to be twenty-two. I was accomplishing more in my twenties than people in their thirties and/or forties were. I had a college degree and finally, I could state that I had a career and not some dead-end job that underpaid and made me unhappy.

Not only could I present to mom that I had gotten the job, but that I also may have found a church home that I sure planned to visit. All that was left from my mother's list of things to accomplish while here in New York was a companion in my life.

Still getting to know who Chris was, my mother would have to temporarily settle for my new career and church visit. A relationship was not priority at the time, but once the time did come it was going to be real and I most certainly had no intentions of hiding from my mother.

No longer in need of the second interview, I respectfully called to cancel as I did not want someone waiting, wondering why I had not shown up. Feeling a bit uneasy about canceling at the last moment, I truly believed God had shown me the place that I was supposed to be and job number two just wasn't it.

Neither one of my parents answering the phone, I left a voicemail, able to release a complete amount of excitement as I sat privately, in my car.

Free for the rest of the day, I retrieved the photo I took on my phone of the church flyer so that I could look up the address and ride past. Not far from my condo, the church certainly captured the attention of a tourist or simply a car passing by. The width and distance of the parking lot, you could tell that there wasn't any empty seat Sunday morning. Pulling in to a parking space, my car now in park, I stopped near the front entrance where I began to read the few flyers on the outside bulletin board.

"Young man, would you like to come inside," said a voice behind me. This voice, so powerful so mighty, you could tell that this man was used to speaking in a public setting.

Leading me into the building, he stopped in the foyer and asked, holding his hands out, "How may I help you son?"

A pro at introducing myself, having done it twice this morning, I took it upon myself to take the lead for the third time today, "My name is Christopher Harris and I just recently moved into town. I stumbled upon your church flyer and wanted to learn more as I am in search of a church home."

Side by side, not sure who I was speaking with, he followed up my introduction with a question of his own, "If you don't mind my asking son, what brings you all the way here to New York?"

Excited to share my journey even more now that I had been hired by an employer, the reason I traveled all this way.

"I came down hoping to jump start my career as I recently graduated from college. By God's grace, here two short days and he blessed me this morning with a job that I already love. Now I'm just looking for a place to worship sir."

His eyes shining bright, he said with much excitement in his voice, "That is awesome son! You have indeed found the right place to worship and praise. We here at *Greater Faith* have held our ministry for over forty-seven years. We seek souls like yourself on a daily basis. I am so glad that you have come to us today and that I was able to meet with you. I am the pastor of this church and I would like to welcome you home son." Just standing in the presence of this here church, I had a great feeling. Even if I decided not to join the church, the rapport that I had with the pastor was enough to guide me into one of the pews Sunday morning.

"Thank you, pastor. What time does service start on

Sunday," I asked.

Quoting this information like the back of his hand, "Bible study begins at ten a.m., service promptly at noon."

Shaking Pastor's firm hand, he left me with a final word as only a pastor would, "Lord willing, I will see you on Sunday son and do not hesitate to bring a guest. You can never bring too many souls to Christ."

Why did I get the impression that the pastor had spoken with my mother? When he asked me to bring someone to church, was he referring to a female? Did everyone want me in a relationship? Was a woman truly going to fulfill my life? I could not catch a break when it came to my nonexistent love life that everyone else was working overtime to exist. The topic presented so many times, I started to wonder myself. If I was going to find that special one, she had to be the woman for me not for everyone else. What I was looking for exactly, I was unsure, but once I found her, I would know.

ROUTINE

I do believe that I was finally used to New York's morning commute hours. A routine developed of ironing my clothing the night before work, eating out only once a week, in effort to stack my bank account which seemed to be working fine.

The job was working out very well also. I had gotten to know Mr. Basketball himself, very well who went by Keenan. The moment I laid eyes on his talent in the gym, I knew he was something special. Reviewing his file, I learned that he and his family were homeless which would explain the expression on his face as well as his everyday appearance. At such an impressionable age, I knew that I could not save everyone in my profession, but I did my very best to offer his family resources to get them back on their feet.

Thanks to dad's generous contribution, I had a check or two that I could use to bless Keenan's family. With my first check, deposited from the center, I purchased shoes for Keenan and his three younger brothers.

In my heart I believed that this job found me for a reason and Keenan was one of those reasons. No father in the home or active male role model, I took him under my wing while in my supervision and worked to instill in him, all that my father instilled within me.

The life of a psychologist was surrounded by both good and bad; happiness and often emotion that we had to hide. Working with these children exposed me to many personal problems; some I could help and others I had to turn over to higher power. My job responsibility called for me to counsel only the children that were brought in by their parents. If the parents did not request a counseling session, I was not allowed to pry. I had broken the barriers between myself and many of the children who confided and believed my word. Used to disappointment, it took a while to get through to many of the children, this barrier, many of my colleagues weren't able to cross. Every Sunday, I carried each child's worry to church with me, laid them across the alter, and prayed that they would see brighter days ahead.

Along with the children, I prayed over my life as well. Everything I sought to accomplish on my own, I had by the grace of God. I could have stayed with mom and dad, but had I done so, I would have never experienced any self-fulfillment brought on by hard work and determination. I began to look back at my life and realized just how blessed I truly was.

For all that I ever complained of as a child, this job humbled me. I was afforded a two-parent home with all of the love and support anyone could imagine where some of these children had to beg for even a hug or kiss. I could have strayed and taken the path many of my friends chose, but my parents never gave up even when I was being a knucklehead.

Every Sunday I also took with me, the heavy burden of Mike's passing. My parents still had no idea how close I came to riding with Mike the night he was murdered. Had it not been for God sparing my life, I would not be here today.

I always found it ironic that every time I stepped into church, the sermon directly spoke to me as if no one else were in the building. On this day, pastor titled his sermon, "Your Better Half."

If that title didn't speak volumes, nothing did.

My mother had pressured me to seek out a Christian woman before moving away. The pastor spoke to me about bringing a guest to church knowing me all of five seconds, and I too, thanks to the persuasion of those near and dear, began to feel lonely walking into a large home, alone. If Jesus himself was not here in the flesh, knocking sense straight into my head, forcing me out of my seat to physically go out and seek my better half.

Sitting in the pew, I wandered off from the sermon a short moment and began evaluating my life now that I was completely settled in NY. Steady income now, I wasn't in fear that I could not financially provide for my queen. Clocking in daily to a job that I was passionate allowed me to come home in a positive light. In a few short months, I had gained many stripes under my belt; I had a college degree, lived on my own, single without children, my job afforded a few luxuries, and I came from a rooted spiritual upbringing that I planned to continue.

All that was missing was her.

CHAPTER SIX

Her

"Her" that stood two rows in front of me on my right. Had my mother been present with me during service, she would have smacked the back of my head for not paying attention and committing the sin of "lust." This woman was beyond beautiful. She had long dark silky hair, a smooth milk chocolate complexion, and the pencil skirt she wore accentuated each and every curve she could not hide.

I did not want to make it obvious that I had my eyes on her, but as beautiful as she was, it was hard to imagine anyone being able to ignore such a work of art. I would not be surprised if I was not physically drooling with my tongue hanging from my mouth which I had never done before, but something about her just wouldn't allow me to be myself. Never had I seen such a woman that caused me to behave in a manner other than that of my usual.

Throughout the sermon, I contemplated whether or not I would introduce myself. Uncertain if she had a companion nearby, I respectfully turned in the opposite direction, my introduction withheld. If it was meant for us to speak, the opportunity would present itself again. If not, I would be fine with that as well for I was not in search of Mrs. Harris, rather a female friend that I could spend time with and get to know. My mind distracted, I had snapped back to reality just as service concluded. The tiny segment I recalled set the entire house on fire, not a soul in their seats.

What I loved about this pastor in comparison to others I had seen and heard, was his ability to touch on topics the entire congregation could relate. He did not dictate, making you feel wrong about your past or attempt to persuade you to feel and/or think a certain way. Instead, his image was that of a true messenger from God sent down to speak the word to his followers. I did not find this church home for it found me and I was glad. Because of this church, I was ready to start my work week off in a positive light.

Having formed a bond in which brother and sister shared, Justine and I had become close. We were able to keep it real with one another whether positive or negative and respect each other's position whether we agreed or disagreed. "Good morning Justine. You look lovely today," in my top of the morning voice.

Using her dainty pitch, she responded filled with laughter, "Why thank you sir. What's on your agenda for the day?"

Completing a double take of Keenan's biweekly progress report, my eyes were glued to his current grades, "Keenan and I are going to have another session. He is falling behind in several subjects and his mother reached out, asking that I speak with him." Taking a deep breath, I knew that motivating Keenan would present difficulty, but I was up for the challenge. "Other than that, I am pretty open. Is there anything you need from me?"

Sitting in Lori's seat, who was out sick for the day, "I'm actually glad that you will be speaking with Keenan. I have noticed a change in his demeanor the last couple of days. He is not the young man that I am used to seeing every day. Maybe you can pull something out of him that no one else can because he certainly disregards what I have to say."

From the moment that I met Keenan, I knew that he would be a challenge; one I was prepared to take on. The thing about speaking with children, you had to show them that you could relate. If you placed blame on them or tried to make them feel bad about any of their chosen actions, they were bound to shut down entirely.

"I will do my very best. I have cleared it with his mother to take him to lunch today. Hopefully a bite to eat will open him up." I could sense that Justine did not believe possible, to establish a breakthrough with Keenan. Blowing air in her cheeks, swooshing each side back and forth, she gave me a thumbs up and said, "Good luck!" In search of Keenan, I began walking the halls assuming I'd find him in the gymnasium.

I too had noticed a difference in him and now that his mother and Justine spoke of it, I had to address our concerns. Just where I thought; I opened the gym door and there he was, hand glued to the ball. His attention captured, I called out, "Keenan, are you ready to go?"

Bouncing the ball two more times on the hardwood floor before taking one final shot at the free throw line, "Yeah." I was trying to teach Keenan proper grammar and found myself consciously correcting what he did not find wrong, "How about yes? What does yeah mean?" Inhaling and exhaling while sluggishly walking towards the door I awaited, "Look, are we gon go or what?"

The attitude everyone had complained about, stared me right in the face and I was not about to let it go unnoticed, "What is with you today?"

"Nuttin," Keenan said, eyebrows raised, idle positioned, awaiting my next move or comment. Holding the door open for him to exit, "Come on Keenan, let's go."

I was so sick of seeing this boy with his pants hanging to his ankles. Not to mention the attitude he displayed in the few short moments that we were together. I was definitely going to get to the bottom of this today.

Watching Keenan complete a half turn with each step he took just to avoid his pants from falling to the ground, I just couldn't take it anymore. Behind him I stood, dizzy just watching him move from side to side, "Boy, pull your pants up." Snapping his head at me, Keenan yanked away at his pant, bringing them no more than a centimeter from the position they were, "It aint cool to wear yo pants to yo waist."

Glancing at his pants, then mine which were at waist level, my eyes repositioned to his again, I asked, "Says who Keenan?"

"It looks like everybody, but you," he joked, laughing to himself. Allowing him this moment for a stand-up comedian act, he received a pass as this was the first time in quite a while that I had seen him crack a smile which meant that progress was being made.

Lightly put, not wanting to dim the light Keenan had surrounding him, I politely schooled this young man on a grown man's style, "Boy, there is nothing wrong with my pants. I have on slacks and they are held up by a belt. No one wants to see your behind. Get in the car."

Frozen at attention, having never seen my car before, Keenan took a moment to stop and stare.

His arms crossed, lips scrunched, touching his nose, Keenan asked, "Is this yo ride? You slangin aint you Mr. Harris?"

Shaking my head at the thought that Keenan believed the only way to obtain valuable items was through the sale of narcotics, "Do you really believe that is the only way to obtain anything nice?"

With a straight face, he responded, "How else you gon pay for this? This job aint payin you shit. I can tell cause the building is broke down and the lunch taste like burnt ass."

In the car, we continued the conversation.

"First of all, I would appreciate it if you would express yourself without cursing at me and the last time I opened a dictionary, the word "aint" and "nuttin" were not included. Second, how do you know how much this job pays me? Third, I work hard for all that I have and I save money. Everything I do is legal, or shall I say, "LEGIT."

Dismissing the conversation, Keenan waved his hand at me as if what I said about my means of living was of false pretense, "Yeah ok."

His mood shifting, I rerouted the conversation, temporarily holding back the discussion of his grades, "How was your weekend?" A heavy breath, Keenan expressed, staring out the window, "Same thang, different day."

Not sure exactly what he meant, I asked, "Would you care to elaborate?" Attitude back in full swing accompanied by a burst of anger, "What man?"

It was behaviors such as Keenan's that easily deterred others from the job title itself. Having a background in developmental psychology, I knew that a breakthrough was drawing near which is why I felt no urgency to give up and throw in the towel on this young man. Meeting Keenan at his own level, I threw a fraction of an attitude back just to give him a taste of his own behavior.

"Are you going to tell me about your day or not man? Did you stare at the wall all weekend," I said, my voice raised slightly. Not used to a challenge, it was at this moment, Keenan broke down, offering a play by play of his weekend. "Mom aint come home all weekend. I couldn't spend any time with my friends cause I had my brothers to watch out for. They were crying because the fridge was empty with only two eggs in the carton and one hard ass piece of cheese. That's how my weekend was. Is that enough for you?"

This moment right here was exactly why I did not

believe in giving up on these kids. Keenan had such weight to carry on his shoulders which explained the frustration he knew only to express by lashing out. He was a young teen who wanted to go out and enjoy time with his friends, but being the oldest, he was often in the position of playing the role of a father where he, himself, did not have one to show him how to overcome many obstacles he was forced to face.

The lines of communication open, I asked, "Is your weekend always like this?"

"Yeah, but I'm used to it," he shrugged.

The last thing I wanted to do was frustrate him further, discussing his grades and behavior in class which is why I decided to stray away from my agenda a bit. We were most definitely going to revisit his grades, but today was not the day. Today, I was going to allow Keenan to make some decisions, "Well today is your special day because I am taking you out to eat."

"You lyin," he said, his eyes big as saucers. A man of my word, I understood Keenan's reservation as he was used to being lied to. Today, I felt I had something to prove which I was going to make every effort. Speaking to him like one of the homies, I said, "I'm for real man. Where do you want to get some grub?"

Unfamiliar with the dance he continued to motion in the passenger seat of my car, I played along, mimicking each move. He said, bouncing his shoulders while rubbing his hand on his stomach in a circular motion, "Oh snap and I'm hungry than a mug. Mikey D's please." His option unlimited, I asked for him to repeat his response, sure that I did not hear the word, McDonald's, "You want to go where?"

"McDonald's." Asking one more time, "Are you sure that's what you want? You can eat there any day."

"You may be able to eat there any day, but not me and my brothers. Besides, their $1 menu is fire."

Unbeknownst of my insensitivity, here I was criticizing where Keenan wanted to go and eat, and this young man was just glad to have an option considering he had not eaten all weekend. Of course, McDonald's was fine for him. I couldn't recall a time where dinner wasn't on the table or in the refrigerator in my home which is why I didn't think before I started poking at his food choice which I felt bad.

There was a lot of work to be done with Keenan; his grades, a top priority. First, before I put any plan into motion, I needed to speak with his mother about there being no food in the home. This was unacceptable and if social services were to ever step in, which I prayed they would not have to, serious action could be taken. I may have been overstepping my boundaries a bit, but in order to aid Keenan, I felt it best to begin with the household which seemed to be where much of his stress stemmed. We needed to work as a team to prepare him for the next grade level. There was great potential in this young man, but with so much on his plate, his focus and drive to succeed was distorted. At his age, he should be out enjoying life; instead, he was left home alone to care for his younger brothers who often cried out of hunger, Keenen helpless, unable to console even himself. Yearning to be nurtured by loving parents who seemed transparent, this too also molded his lack of openness. He was not living the life of a teenager, but that of a grown man and in some form, a father with a responsibility that was not his own.

Throughout the week, Keenan and I spent a lot of time in the center's library perfecting his speech and preparing his mind for the next level. He was going into high school in the fall and I wanted to prepare him as much as possible for the journey ahead. This also meant building his confidence.

Today's generation, so worried about the next kid's exterior appearance added an additional layer of worry to

Keenan's stress level. Due to his circumstances at home, he was not afforded much which may make it hard for him to keep connected with the latest fashions especially entering high school. A family of four boys who all depended on their single mother, they were lucky to get even one new outfit to start the school year. Working three dead end jobs not even equivalent to one steady source of income, there was no extra money. I often went home with Keenan heavy on my heart. There was a limit to what I could do for him, but there was no limit to prayer.

CHAPTER SEVEN

We Meet Again

In the blink of an eye, Sunday had returned which meant that it was time to worship with my Greater Faith family. I could always count on the ushers placing me front and center of the sanctuary which was definitely a switch in gears compared to the many years I attended church with my mother and father.

Entering the sanctuary back home as a family of three, we often found ourselves in the back of church filled with an atmosphere of late comers, those suffering from a hangover, some who'd overslept, others struggling to keep their eyes open having just clocked out from third shift, while the rest were on the verge of a breakdown in need of healing.

I had learned the secret to ownership of a front row seat which consisted of two things; one, you had to arrive on time and two, enter into the house of the Lord, party of one. That combination there, no chance on earth you could avoid the eye contact of the front row usher who would come and get you if you even thought to stray and intermingle in the middle or back pew. He or she was more than glad to wave you in the direction of the front. This here spot, no way you could avoid eye contact with pastor which meant you had better be alert, paying full attention.

On this particular Sunday, I happened to be seated second row from the front.

Directed to stand as Deacon John read the response scripture, my nose captured a sweet, mesmerizing scent from the woman who stood front and center of my eyesight.

After joining together in scripture, it was time for the congregation to extend a hand of fellowship to those near and far in the sanctuary. Disbursed, moved by the spirit that filled the room, I trailed up and down the aisles interlocking hands with those I had become familiar others I was introduced for the first time. Back to my seat, my eyes froze, the sight in front of me far beyond breathtaking.

It was "her" again wearing the color red for the second time and I must say, red was certainly her color. Unable to remove my eyes from her true beauty, I stood in amazement as the lights from the ceiling placed a halo around every inch of her body. Discreetly slapping my midsection, praying to God that it would retreat back to a normal appearance as church was about to conclude, I found it impossible to keep my eyes from the very sight that had me intrigued.

My hands forming an X in front of me, I found myself in a traffic jam, the ushers releasing one row at a time upon conclusion of service. The front row dismissed, I stepped out following the hand signal of the usher. Focusing down at my midsection, I exited the pew paying no attention, running right into the side of Ms. Beautiful herself.

Apologetic I was, fearing I may have wounded her, for once in my life I found someone other than myself leading the conversation. I could feel the saliva forming in my mouth preparing to pour from my lips as I stood in close proximity of an angel who had my senses confused.

Holding her hand out, she said in such a soothing tone, "Good morning! My name is Mackenzie."

Mackenzie. That name rang throughout my entire body. Knocking some sense into the scared little boy within, I quickly channeled the man in me in fear I would miss the opportunity to acquaint myself with Ms. Mackenzie. Reaching for her hand, "It's nice to meet you. My name is Christopher."

Our greeting temporarily stopping the flow of traffic, I found myself in a trance watching her eyes twinkle.

Never in my entire life had I been so nervous and out of character to speak to a female. My boys back home would have ate this moment up, talking about me for days. She wasn't your average female though. When she walked, she held her head high, her strut that of a queen demanding respect from her onlookers. When she spoke, so fluent, proper, and mellifluous, you couldn't help, but to give all of your attention.

This being our second encounter, this more formal than the last, I was quite certain that she was alone and without the company of another. Now, if I could muster up the courage to ask her out to dinner without stumbling over my words or making a complete fool out of myself, I could crown this day a success.

Single since freshman year of college, I was a bit rusty when it came to pursing a woman. I wanted Mackenzie bad and little did she know, I was coming for her. Blowing the dust off of my tucked away charm that had been put away for a spell, I positioned myself for what I hoped would be a victory.

CHAPTER EIGHT

Make A Move

An elderly woman excusing herself into the very aisle we stood side by side, Mackenzie and I found our new-found conversation broken. For every step the elderly woman took with the aid of a walker, Mackenzie grew further and further into the distance. Wanting so bad to lift the woman and her walker from the floor and gently move her to the side, I respectfully waited, wondering if this distraction was a sign from God to keep both Mackenzie and I apart.

Focusing much on the elderly woman who trailed slowly in front of me while others stepped to the side to ease in front of her, I looked up to find Mackenzie had vanished and so too had my opportunity to extend an invitation to dinner.

Beating myself slightly, I headed out into the parking lot towards my car. Here I was allowing others to impact me into truly believing that I needed someone to be with when God was clearly showing me that I didn't. The second time I had lost focus, I repositioned my head above my shoulders in enough time to notice a Lexus heading towards me at full speed.

Holding my hands out, pleading with the driver to stop, I began to breath heavy, my heart practically jumping out of my chest. Hidden behind tinted windows, I could not see clearly, the driver of the car. Car in park, I awaited their appearance outside of the car before expressing my frustration for their lack of care for pedestrians in the parking lot, myself specifically.

What was wrong with this driver?

The lack of urgency to get out of the car infuriated me and I let them know, keeping in mind that I had just stepped out of church, "Dang it. You could have killed me." The driver side window lowering at a very slow rate, no one in sight, I walked over towards the side of the car and you would never guess the identity of the driver; her again.

Looking up to the sky, I thought, God sure had a sense of humor; this time, however, he was hardly funny. Had anyone else been in the driver seat you better believe I would have continued expressing myself in an unpleasant tone.

"I'm so sorry Chris," she said, placing her hand on her chest.

She almost killed me, but how could I be mad, I mean it was Mackenzie?

Reintroduced at the hands of a near death experience, location still was not on our side as her car and my body stood in a high traffic area of the parking lot. Frustrated drivers began to sound their horns, those without air in their cars began to shout through the window out of frustration and those overcome by hunger pains began to stare with a look like, if she didn't run you over with her car we were going to run you over with ours.

Using this moment of distress to my advantage as she almost ran me over, I requested that she follow me to my car so that we could continue our conversation, free from oncoming traffic.

Placing my hands on the frame of her door, I leaned in, asking, "Would you mind following me to my car?"

"Sure," she responded.

Fearing she may actually hit me, Mackenzie kept a great

distance between myself and her car as she followed me. Pointing to my car, she parked one space over. Standing in between her Lexus and my Charger, I knelt down, released my fear, and asked one very important question.

Playing in my head, what is meant to be will be, I swallowed my pride and asked, "Would you mind having dinner with me? I know we don't know each other outside of a hand shake, but I would really like to learn about Mackenzie."

My eyebrows raised in effort to read her facial expressions, I sensed slight hesitation as she possibly had options to weigh. As beautiful as she was, I wouldn't doubt she had men banging down her front door. She was probably overwhelmed by the number of requests she received on a day to day basis.

Rubbing the steering wheel with the palms of her hands, she looked at me and stared while biting down on her bottom lip. I felt the word "no" drawing near as I stood from the ground, my legs growing tired. Halfway off the ground, my legs buckled, an act I tried to hide as my ears heard a faint, "Where to?" In my mind I was thinking, hell yes! In not so many words Mackenzie had agreed to have dinner with me and I was elated. Using the guidance given by my father on how to treat a woman, I allowed Mackenzie to select where we ate.

"Seeing that I'm new to the area, I'm not too familiar with the restaurants around town. Do you have any recommendations?"

There wasn't one nonverbal Mackenzie displayed that didn't leave a lasting impression. Even sitting in the car, thinking of where to go, she was breathtaking.

"There is a nice restaurant called Nixon Square."

Removing her palm from the steering wheel, she pointed her index finger to the right and said, "It's a couple of blocks up the road if that works for you."

She could have selected a restaurant in Africa and that would have been fine if I was in her presence.

Attempting to contain my excitement, I said in the most composed tone that I could, "That sounds perfect. I'll follow you."

With a smile on her face, "Ok."

Trailing behind Mackenzie, I couldn't believe that she actually agreed to have dinner with me. I felt like I just hit the lotto. Now, if only I could hold an interesting conversation long enough to keep her entertained.

Nixon Square a few blocks up the road, we had arrived in under ten minutes. I placed my car in park, just in front of the restaurant where I adjusted the rearview mirror to check certain features the eye was prone to glance. Grabbing the brush from my center console, I gave my head a few strokes forward even though I had just gone to a barber three short days ago. I followed the strokes, rubbing the hairs forward to make sure not one strand stood out of place. Flaring my nostrils up and out, I checked each for any unwelcoming visitors that I'm certain, would be an immediate turn off. Opening my mouth, I checked between each tooth, searching for food remnants. Cuffing my hands, I offered a tiny sample of my breath, and although in decent order, I saw no reason not to spray a couple shots of binaca. Finally, one squirt of Polo cologne and I felt secure enough to exit the car and stand before a queen.

A few steps ahead as always, I ran behind Mackenzie in effort to grab hold of the door before she even thought to use a muscle, letting herself into the building. You were not a man if you allowed a woman to open a door for herself and I stood firm on that belief. Behind her I stood where the hostess grabbed two menus and prepared to seat us asking, "Will it be just the two of you?" Holding in my amusement, thinking of Will Smith's song, "just the two of us," I shook my head, happily confirming, "Yes ma'am."

Seated at our table, I expressed my appreciation for Mackenzie agreeing to have dinner with me, "I thought I was going to have to have dinner by myself. Thank you for joining me!"

Her eyes glued to the menu which covered half of her face, she giggled and responded, "A girl has to eat."

Looking up in laughter, she added, removing the menu from her face, "I'm just playing. It is a pleasure. I have been watching you make eye contact with me for some time. What took you so long?" Here I was thinking I kept enough distance that she couldn't see me drooling over her and she noticed the entire time. Slightly embarrassed, using the menu as a crutch to conceal my face, I attempted to buy myself some time coming up with the perfect response to Mackenzie outing my methods of watching her.

Dismissing the fact that she knew I was watching her, I focused only on her question of my urgency to approach her, "To be honest, I didn't know if you were with anyone and wanted to wait it out until I knew for sure before approaching you."

Unmoved by my response, she followed up, "Why didn't you just ask?" If only she knew how much courage it took to get to this day or the fact that I wanted to jump across the table, reach for her face, and lay kisses all over her. I held my hands out as I often did when passionately speaking, "I'm a man who takes his time. I don't like rushing in to anything I do."

Throwing a similar question to Ms. Mackenzie, "Since we are on the subject, if you noticed me noticing you, why didn't you say anything Miss Lady?"

From her facial expression, this question had Mackenzie in a state of shock. Laying the menu face down, she placed both of her hands on the table and responded, "Women are not supposed to go after men thank you very much." Disagreeing completely with her thought process, I gave this beautiful, misinformed lady, a history lesson, "It's 2018. Women are getting pretty bold. I mean they are even getting down on one knee to propose. There aren't too many waiting around for men to come chasing after them."

"Look who made the first move here Mr. 2018," she said, smiling, pointing her finger at me. Laughter ensued amongst the two of us as we both stood firm on our positions, neither of us backing down. It was beyond hard to take my eyes away from her beauty. The more she spoke, the longer I stared.

Giving Mackenzie the floor to order first as the waitress returned with our drinks, I used the period in which we awaited our food to dive into who Mackenzie was outside of a beautiful work of God. Parched, I reached for my glass of water, took a long, refreshing sip and allowed my questions to flow however they chose to come. "So, what do you do for a living?"

As if she had practiced this response, she said quick and with much passion, "I am a traveling nurse." Now I had heard of LPN's and RN's, but traveling nurses, now that was a new one.

"I've never heard the term traveling nurse before. Do you enjoy traveling?" Displaying the cutest Kool-Aid smile, she announced, "I enjoy it very much! I get to meet new people and I love going state to state, exposing myself to new scenery."

Asking the same of me, "What is it that you do Mr. Christopher?"

Wanting not to bore her with my lengthy story, I cut out all of the minor details and kept the response short and sweet, "I just moved to town a couple of months ago after graduating college. I work as a counselor at a youth center."

"Now that takes patience. Do you enjoy what you do," she asked while lifting her chair forward, intrigued by my profession.

Moving forward myself, I felt Mackenzie had just given me the green light to in fact elaborate, "Very much so. I was afforded many opportunities that these children are not, and I just want to give back. The challenge does come having to hide my emotional side. Some of what these children have gone through or are currently forced to endure, is often hard to process. They have lots of trust issues which makes getting close often complicated. Some I can get through to, while others, well, it's just going to take time." Taking a deep breath in, slowly releasing, "Wow. I know, I, myself would find it nearly impossible to hold my emotions in. How do you manage to compose yourself?"

Now that question had me tongue tied as I'd never been asked that before. How was I able to keep my feelings buried? Thinking of children like Keenan who went days without a decent meal, I found myself in a compromising position where as a man, I did not want to display my tears.

Men were able to hurt, but expressing and displaying our pain on an external level, now that was not of us.

Answering her question as best I could, "Honestly, each case is different. With some, I can hold it in; others, I have to excuse myself from the atmosphere at times. What I want these kids to know and understand is that it is ok to break down and release all that bothers them, we just have to work on the methods used so that we are not destructive." I had allowed my heart to speak this response and whether or not it satisfied for Mackenzie, it was all that I had to give.

Out of nowhere, Mackenzie reached across the table and placed her hand on top of mine. Our eyes aligned with one another, she spoke life into my soul, giving her opinion of the response I had to offer. "I believe that it takes a special person to do this line of work. Those children are blessed to have such a dedicated counselor who clearly loves them." Her words really made me think. I was devoted to these children, had their best interest at heart, and wanted to see them succeed, but never had I placed in my head that I loved them until speaking with Mackenzie today.

She had put my bond with these children into perspective and helped me see that I did love them and for that, I was appreciative, "Thank you Mackenzie!"

Our food arrived, we exchanged laughter back and forth while indulging in each other's plate. On several occasions I caught a glimpse of Mackenzie checking the dance floor out which I tried not to make obvious. The music had a nice melody and made anyone want to get out of their seat and dance except for me. Now, I did have a mean bounce, but I was not one to slow dance which seemed to be the only dancing that took place on the center floor.

Trying so hard not to stare, even a stranger could see how bad Mackenzie wanted to get out on the dance floor, I mean she no longer had any interest in her dinner plate and her body began to sway side to side no matter what song played. Taking a deep breath against better judgment, I rose from my seat, patting my mouth with a napkin, walked over to Mackenzie and held my hand out into the air while asking, "May I have this dance?" Guided on the floor by Luther Vandross as the DJ dimmed the lights, Mackenzie and I interlocked fingers as we slow danced to *A House is Not a Home.*

Respectfully keeping my distance, I let Mackenzie take the lead on each and every movement our bodies made. Not twenty seconds into the song, she leaned in close and asked, "Do you have two left feet Mr. Christopher?"

And there it was, my secret was out, "Let's just say that

I haven't touched a dance floor in years."

Pulling me in, Mackenzie became my dance instructor. We were now toe to toe, chest to chest further enjoying the company of one another. Her hand in mine, mine in hers, we allowed the music to carry us away into our own fairytale and I prayed that inside of her mind, she was enjoying this evening as much as I. Our food now ice cold, Mackenzie and I had spent four nonstop hours on the dance floor and as much as I did not want to see her go, it was time for us both to part.

Holding the door open as she stepped out of the restaurant, I escorted Mackenzie to her car. With every step, I contemplated whether or not to kiss her. In the driver seat she sat as I held the door open, not sure what to say or do.

The engine started, her soft and beautiful hand on the interior of the driver side door, I felt my time winding down and still I could not act or speak. Taking the advice of 2018 females, Mackenzie surprised me offering her phone number which I was more than willing to accept, exchanging mine.

"I had so much fun Chris! I'll be on the road the next couple of weeks, but I do look forward to seeing you again." Even though she was standing before me at this very moment, I could not wait to see her again. Two weeks was two weeks too long.

CHAPTER NINE

What Are You Doing To Me

Now I was nowhere near sprung, but I just could not get Mackenzie off of my mind. Thinking of her made me also think of my mother whom I had not yet informed that I had gone on my first date with a CHURCH GIRL as she would say.

I mean, we had only gone on one date and I did not want to get my mother's hopes up. Lord knows if I uttered the words date, church, and female, she would have my entire wedding planned. If Mackenzie and I went further than one date and a few texts here and there, I would certainly enlighten my parents, but until then, I would hold on to my little secret and simply daydream about her while at work.

Although my date was amazing, it did not distract me from reaching out to Keenan as I made sure to do each and every weekend when out of my sight. He was a diehard Cavs fan and even though I found the team overrated, I had no problem engaging in harmless debate with my buddy. A fan of Golden State myself, Keenan made sure to always tell me how bad of a team they were and that the Cavs could outscore them any day. After speaking with him, I completed my day on the patio, listening to Pandora, watching the sun go down. Preparing my mind for the week ahead all I saw when I looked out to the sky was Mackenzie. All I heard on my Pandora, Luther Vandross. Retreating to my bedroom, taking the thought of Mackenzie with me, I sat my phone on the nightstand, climbed into my bed, and closed my eyes for a good night's sleep which was short lived, the text alert on my phone sounding off.

Thinking twice about opening my eyes, I was sunk deep into the mattress, my eyes heavy, and I knew that if I removed myself from the state that I was in, there was no turning back. Knowing it was either my mother or Keenan, I forfeited my relaxing position, turned my lights back on in the bedroom, and looked at my phones message log. Yawning aloud while rubbing my eyes to gain a better visual of my phones screen, my eyes began to bat in a rhythmic motion, a reaction to the sender.

Grateful that I decided to wake up, as much as I was thinking of Mackenzie she was obviously thinking of me enough to send a text which read, "Thank you for dinner this evening! I cannot wait to see you in two weeks."

Wanting desperately to respond, I did not want it to come off that I had my phone glued to my fingertips just waiting on her text. I would certainly respond to her text, but unfortunately, it would have to wait until sunrise.

Thinking that I was not going to be able to fall back to sleep, interrupted by my phone, it was Mackenzie's text along with the memory of our afternoon and evening shared that cradled me to sleep like an infant wrapped in a swaddling blanket.

NEXT MORNING

I had my morning routine down; arise at 6:20 a.m., compliments of my phones alarm, head to the kitchen to heat up my Keurig, relax in a hot shower while I allowed my morning cup of joe to brew, suit up in the clothing I prepared the night before, and out the door, carrying with me a productive mindset to conquer the day. Not at all forgetting, I had to respond to Mackenzie's text message, but how?

I did not want to say too much, but I also did not want

to appear short in conversation as if I were brushing her off like some random female I had no interest in further seeing. Back and forth, trying to figure out what to say exactly felt as if I were in the front seat of class, unprepared for an exam. I probably spent about ten minutes typing and erasing my response.

Hoping my words weren't too much or too little, I left her with, "Anytime. Have a nice work week." Placing the phone in my back pocket which barely hit the bottom stitching, Mackenzie was responding which sparked our day to day dialogue.

All week I stepped into work, my vibe untouchable. I was smiling from ear to ear and loving life. Our daily texts knocked me off my feet as Stevie Wonder would say. Her words, although short and random throughout the day, I kept in my mind that she was a traveling nurse which did not allow a lot of personal time. I was grateful to even have a line of communication no matter what time of day.

"Mr. Harris, why do you have that goofy grin on yo face," Keenan asked as I approached him in the gym.

"What grin," as I tried to play it off.

Inappropriately asking, "Did you get some last night?"

This boy had absolutely no filter when it came to the words he chose.

On a high you could not remove me, I ignored Keenan's question and proceeded with the day. Bouncing the ball, Keenan added, "That look on yo face is straight corny. You only see that face on two people; someone who just won some bread or someone who just hit it." His conversation which surpassed any subject of fourteen-years-old, I could not speak for I was lost in strong like for a woman I could not get off of my mind.

"I'm just being real with you," he said, obviously forgetting that he was supposed to be in the library, working on a history paper which I gladly escorted him, gently guiding his neck with the palm of my hand out the door and towards the correct room he was to report.

Keeping him up to speed with his agenda, "Boy, let's go to the library. You have a test this week. That is the only focus you should have at this time. If you analyzed your books the way you analyze my personal life, we are sure to see some A's on that next report card, right?"

While getting Keenan on track, I started to wonder if I needed to get myself on track as well. Was I really cheesing that hard? If anyone was going to speak truth, it most certainly was Keenan and he seemed to think that I was different in appearance and I could not lie, maybe I was.

Only one date and I was all over the place with happiness which wasn't a bad thing, but never had I experienced this out of body feeling with any female, but Mackenzie. What was this girl doing to me?

CHAPTER TEN

Are You Sure

No one on earth could kill the vibe that surrounded me. For the past hour in between text messages Mackenzie and I sent back and forth, I began to sing Tony Toni Tone's, "Do you know what today is," in my head.

It wasn't the celebration of an anniversary, but still a celebratory moment. Today marked two weeks that Mackenzie had been gone and in spite of electronically communicating, I still felt incomplete without her presence.

She had the nerve to ask via text, "Do you miss me?" I wanted to respond, "What kind of silly ass question is that?" Hell yes I missed her.

Refraining from using profanity to communicate my feelings, to her question I responded with a question of my very own, "Do you even have to ask Mackenzie?"

Sitting on the couch, getting ready to watch the Cavs vs. Golden State, I had just ended my phone conversation with Keenan and man, was he full of slick things to say about Golden State. Placing a small bet on the game; if my team won, he owed me a B+ or better on his final which meant that he had to put forth much effort. If his team won, I owed him a trip to Taco Bell which I swore to myself, I would not criticize this time around.

Glancing at the time on my phone, I noticed an unread text message from Mackenzie. Consumed by back and forth smack talk with Keenan over the phone, I must have overlooked her message she had sent seventeen minutes ago. "What are you doing this evening," she asked.

I wanted to respond, "Thinking of you."

I stated instead, "I just ordered a pizza and I'm getting ready to watch the game."

The message she sent next, had a brother FEENIN like *Jodeci,* "That sounds relaxing. Would you like some company?" Despite sending a text message only, I still found myself tongue tied, not sure how to go about responding to her message. Of course, she could join me, but my fingers were frozen, unable to convey that message. This moment which I could not move nor speak was either my mother's sabotage or God telling me no. Now I loved them both, I swear I did, but tonight, I was listening to self only. Whatever the repercussion, I'd deal with later.

"Would you like to join me," I responded.

No response in return, I feared that I may have scared Mackenzie off asking her to join me. I knew that at some point I was going to make a mistake, saying the wrong thing. It appeared that God and my mother had won after all. Leaning back on the couch, arms crossed, lips pouting with a mellow mood, I reconvened watching the game by myself. Golden State down by seventeen, this night just couldn't get any worse. I'd scared the woman I was interested in away and now I was going to lose a bet to a fourteen-year-old. Tell me how my night was going to get any better than this.

Embracing a momentary manly hissy fit, I threw my phone on the opposite end of the couch where I heard it make a sound. Sluggishly reaching across the couch, I was not at all interested in hearing Keenan gloat about his team being in the lead. Nervous to open the message for it was not Keenan rather Mackenzie. Wanting to rebuild our line of communication, I gathered up enough courage to read Mackenzie's response which would also shed light on any further interaction we may or may not have.

"You want me to come to your house," she asked.

So that there was no misunderstanding, I made it clear to her that I planned to be the perfect gentleman. "Yes, if you'd like. I promise to keep my hands to my side."

Not sure if she took my word that I planned to be a gentleman, I could see through my phone that she was in the process of writing a message, but had not yet sent it.

After three minutes she responded, "I won't be interrupting anything will I? I mean you won't have any other visitors, will you?"

I found humor in Mackenzie's indirect questions. What she really wanted to know is if I were seeing anyone else. Little did she know, she was the only one I had my eyes on. I may have been cautious on what I said to her, but I had no problem making it very clear that she had nothing or no one to worry about. "You have no one else to worry about. You're the only one I want to see."

I sent my response wondering if I had just placed myself in the "common male phrase" club that many men responded when in fact they were seeing other women. Unbothered, she asked, "Would you like for me to bring anything?"

I appreciated her offer, but there was nothing she could bring that could compare to her presence in my home.

"Unless you're not a fan of pizza, just bring yourself."

Her humorous personality displayed through text, "Who does not like pizza? You have got to get to know me Chris."

"Well come see me," I said.

"What is your address," she inquired.

Excited to see her, I took one look around my house and

panicked. Although I had not used my home as a bachelor pad as my mother worried and Mackenzie assumed, I did sort of use it as a garbage disposal.

I had less than twenty minutes to straighten up and dispose of any visible trash that made a home throughout the four walls of my condo. Thank goodness for Febreze and cabinets I could store trash where she would not find.

A quick shower, Pandora running through the speakers of my home, a bottle of wine chilling in the refrigerator; we were all set for what I hoped would be a pleasant evening for Mackenzie and I to further acquaint ourselves.

Halfway in the shower, the water just barely hitting my right side, I could hear the doorbell ring. Fearing she would leave if I kept her waiting too long, I turned off the water, and stepped out of the tub as fast as I could.

"I'll be right there," I shouted, attempting to catch my balance.

Quickly thinking, was I going to wear a button-down shirt or dress down in basketball shorts and t-shirt?

Nearly tangling my legs together, I ran to the front door as fast as I could, wanting Mackenzie to wait no longer.

Reintroduced to the physical exterior of her existence and I found myself mesmerized all over again. Still beautiful as ever, it seemed that her beauty had further enhanced having been apart for two long weeks.

Honing in on the saying, "absence makes the heart grow fonder," I was left speechless, her absence making my heart pump through my chest. Taking one look at me, she stepped forward, rubbing left over water I had forgotten to remove while speed drying myself off, "How can you be wet and I haven't even touched you yet?" In disbelief that she was standing at my front door, her comment, a sexual innuendo, went straight over my head.

"I was just getting out of the shower when you rang the doorbell. I apologize for keeping you waiting." Pinching a portion of my shirt with both her thumb and index finger, Mackenzie pulled me close and asked while sniffing, "Are you fresh now?"

"I do believe so," I secretly sniffed as if she knew something I didn't.

"Well may I have a hug," she requested, her arms outstretched. Taking in her scent as I brought my nose towards the side of her neck, she smelled like heaven. The amount of perfume she wore wasn't overpowering and accompanied her very well. The scent appeared strongest as I crossed paths with her shoulder, neck, and right ear lobe.

That's it. I had taken the bait, bit down on the worm, and like a fish, I was hooked on Mackenzie.

Inviting her in like a gentleman should, her eyes lit bright and with a gasp of air, she smiled and said, "Chris, your home is beautiful!"

Her compliments intensifying my strong like for her, I let my guard down completely, no longer afraid to be myself in her presence. "Thank you!"

Extending my arm out, I asked, "Would you like a tour?"

"Really," she asked with a bright smile on her face.

Thank goodness there were only two occupied rooms; the living room and my bedroom. That made the cleanup process that much faster prior to her arrival.

Holding on to my arm, I escorted her throughout my home. With a visual of four doors of which only one was open for display, Mackenzie's curiosity aided her to inquire, "If it's just you, why do you have four bedrooms?" Displaying a tiny resemblance of my mother's inquisitiveness, I felt optimistic that Mackenzie and I were going to get along great.

Breaking down to Mackenzie what she had made up in her mind as either an impulse buy or hidden agenda, I explained the idle rooms in my home, "At the time I leased the condo, there wasn't a single one bedroom available and they were having a hard time leasing their four bedrooms. The special they ran for this one," I said, looking around my home, "I couldn't pass up."

Holding on to her hand which remained pressed against my arm, I took Mackenzie to what I believed was the highlight of my home.

Guiding her down the hall and past the kitchen, for a split second I broke our interlocked arms, pulled back the blinds, and unlocked the patio door. "You haven't seen anything until you check out this view."

I held her hand as she stepped out onto the patio. With one step that could easily be missed, I remained close to Mackenzie as she slowly pranced around in her black stilettos.

"Wow," she said holding onto the balcony railing. "You can see the entire city Chris," she smiled, looking back at me.

Nodding my head in agreement, "It is nice, isn't it? This is my chill spot. I come out here to clear my mind and unwind from the work day."

Resting on the opposite end of the balcony as myself, Mackenzie asked, "What are you clearing your mind of?"

Using the railing as a backrest, I crossed my arms, releasing my many thoughts in which Mackenzie expressed concern. "Stories the kids tell me at the center, my mother stressing me out about settling down, and silly things I often let get to me." Yearning for more, Mackenzie continued, "Why is your mother in such a rush for you to settle down?"

Rocking my head back and forth, "You would have to ask her that question. I want to get married at some point, but right now I want to establish myself as a man."

Looking around at how far I had come thus far, I was proud of myself, but knew there was much more that I was capable of. "This is my first home all to myself that I am enjoying. I've had my job only three months, nowhere near long enough to stack and save. I honestly cannot even say that I've encountered someone special enough to take that next step."

With a slight shift in mood, Mackenzie asked sarcastically, "What do you consider me Chris?"

Afraid of answering that question wrong, I asked very timid, "As far as what?"

"Am I not special to you," she asked, releasing her arms to the side.

Lifting from my rested position, my arms released to their side, I leaned in close to explain, "I like you Mackenzie and that is something that I cannot deny no matter how hard I try. Of course, you are special, very special."

A radiant smile back on display, I blew a sigh of relief as Mackenzie responded, "I like you too Chris."

The sun now set, a chilly breeze placing our contact close to one another, we stood silent, lost in an intimate gaze. Catching the cutest quiver vibrate from Mackenzie's bottom lip, I guided our conversation back inside of the house with her permission of course.

"Would you like to go inside and watch the game with me?"

Rubbing her arms up and down, she responded, "Sure."

Modeling that of a true gentleman, I bared witness to each and every construction God blessed Mackenzie's body with, a view I was thankful to have a front row seat. Of no enhancement at all, her back side was extremely healthy. It was round, firm, so enticing that I had to withstand the urge to help myself to a touch and feel session.

Inviting her over to the couch where she sat and I stood, I stepped up my hosting duties, offering Mackenzie a beverage, "Would you like a glass of wine?"

Gracefully responding with an intrigued appearance, "That would be nice."

The simple task of pouring two glasses of wine I found nearly impossible, both glasses running over. Distracted by Mackenzie who added life into my living room as if she'd been here before, my mind began to make me believe that just maybe this was where she belonged.

Both glasses in my hand, I joined Mackenzie on the couch where she commented, "I wouldn't take you for a wine drinker Chris." She was actually correct. I wasn't a drinker at all. The only reason I even had a bottle in my house was because John gave it to me as a welcoming gift.

Not one to front or pretend, I revealed how this very bottle which I must say, added a relaxing vibe to the evening, came to be. "You're exactly right. It's very rare that I have a drink in hand. This bottle," I said, indulging in a small sip, "was a gift from my realtor."

The two of us babysitting our half empty glasses, I recalled that I had a container of strawberries in the fridge which would add further excitement to this beautiful evening.

Three cushions available on the couch; left, middle, right and like two scared children, I occupied the far left while she sat on the far right, the middle cushion dividing us.

I found it funny that our conversations via text brought us extremely close to one another. We would talk for an hour at a time, the subject matter deeply rooted into our personal lives and strangely enough, given the opportunity to sit before one another and no more than a random sentence did either of us express. We were familiar strangers in public and what appeared, distant lovers electronically.

Patting on the middle cushion, I asked, reaching for her hand, "Why are you sitting so far away Miss Mackenzie?"

My words used against me, Mackenzie recalled our conversation via text, refreshing my memory, "Now you did say that you were going to keep this night G rated, remember?"

"You're right, I did say that," slowly pulling my hand back.

Mackenzie's fingers inching towards the middle cushion, she warned, "The closer I get to you the higher we'll have to change tonight's rating." Up for the challenge, without hesitation, I allowed my hand to interact with hers as it laid lonely and still. Comforting her hand with a soft and gentle rub, "I promise I will not overstep my boundaries."

Going with the flow of the evening, continuing in conversation, our hands remained interlocked together as if they'd never been apart.

Taking the lead, Mackenzie asked, "What do you think of New York so far?"

"I enjoy it! My job, well you know I love it. My neighbors, pretty chill. What I love most," looking into her eyes, laying a finger on her chin, "I met you."

"I'd be lying if I said that I did not miss my home town, but New York has shown me so much love. I don't miss home as bad as I did when I first relocated. I do have to admit," barrier down, unafraid to hide my feelings any longer.

Neck outstretched, ears pointing high, Mackenzie aided my confession, "Yes Chris." Placing my palm on top of her hand, staring deep into her eyes with the hopes of easing into her soul, "I missed you so much while you were away."

Would this revelation come off as thirsty? Was I moving too fast? I did not know the answer nor did I care, all I knew was that I did not want any regrets, wondering what I could have or should have said to make her see that she had me hooked.

Before I could finish the thoughts that flowed through my head, I was interrupted by Mackenzie's body which lifted from a distant cushion to the one which sat next to me. Her hands cuffed, she leaned in close. A cool minty breeze tickling my ear drum with a soft whisper of, "What if I said I missed you more?"

So many desires I wanted to act upon with an internal hinderance that held me back. A hinderance I wanted to slap upside the head. A hinderance that had me shackled and bound, without room to break free and place action to the words both Mackenzie and I shared.

Mackenzie right by my side, as much as I had examined her on the exterior surface, I still found myself intrigued with her internal which I took myself on a quest to learn more of. "Tell me something I don't already know about you? Who is Mackenzie really?" As if I had just positioned her in the hot seat, Mackenzie relocated back to the farthest cushion, the distance in between us again. Her shoes removed, she lifted her freshly manicured toes up and rested them underneath her behind as if she were preparing to take me on a journey into her life which I was ready for the ride.

Clearing her throat, the ride had begun, "Mackenzie is a

traveling nurse as you know. I am twenty-five. I graduated from Spelman College with a degree in nursing. I am single with no children. I love to have a good time and in any relationship, all I ask for is honesty."

My selective hearing in full swing, I could hear nothing she stated, but the omission that she was in fact, single.

Lights flashing, a choir of angels descended from heaven and all I heard, HALLELUJAH in such a harmonious tone.

As excited as I was to learn that I had an opportunity to make her mine, I could not help, but to wonder which I asked, "I have to ask, why in the world are you single? You have everything going for you and no one has made you their wife yet?"

"Do you see a ring on this finger," wiggling her fingers up in the air.

Overcome with excitement, I passionately tucked my bottom lip in, just thinking of all the things I'd like to do if Mackenzie were truly mine. "These New York men are slacking out here to let a diamond like you go by. I would have married you long ago and made love to you each and every night like it was our first time." Molding my top teeth into my bottom lip, if I could hear the words my inner thoughts said, surely Mackenzie could which was not the goal.

"Did I just say that out loud," a question I already knew the answer, but was banking on a different response.

What was I thinking? I could not believe I just said all of that.

Instead of collecting her shoes and purse walking right out of the door, she instead drew closer, this time, grabbing my arm and positioning it around her shoulder.

Mackenzie was the crowned captain of this here ship.

Whatever direction she moved, I imitated. Testing the waters completely, I arched her chin up slightly and with my lips, I placed a kiss onto hers which tempted me from the second she stepped inside of my home.

The kiss so passionate yet startling at the same time, like a bolt of lightning, the two of us flew back to our starting point cushions where we both sat in silence, uncertain of what the other was thinking. Playing peek-a-boo with our eyes, I jokingly said, "I see you staring at me. I also see that you had no problem turning our night way beyond G rated either."

Pointing the finger at her chest, Mackenzie asked, "Who me? I'm more than willing to extend much of the credit to you sir."

In laughter I stood, grabbing the wine glasses, now empty, "Can I get you anything else?" Resting comfortably on the couch, Mackenzie's response, "No thank you. Just hurry back."

The kitchen, my temporary home due to the visible erection, too stubborn to return to its original state. Temptation high, in spite of wanting my male part to calm down, her presence aroused him which he had no problem exposing his excitement. Occupying the kitchen longer than the average person simply rinsing two wine glasses, Mackenzie become curious, "Do you need help in their Chris?"

Yes I needed help, but it wasn't the kind that she could assist with. Little did she know, her beauty and presence in my home was making the matter worse. Respectfully declining her offer, I shouted, "I'm fine."

I couldn't recall ever having an erection that lasted this long and I became worried that it may never return to its original. Hunched over, I gave my friend down under several taps hoping to correct my external problem, but this did nothing. Footsteps growing louder in sound, I looked up to find

Mackenzie no longer on the couch, but coming towards the kitchen I was currently occupying as an escape route.

Crossing my hands in an X form in front of me, praying she would not get the wrong impression, I stood tall and as best as I could, pretended nothing was going on.

The one time that I needed her to stay back, she wouldn't. Sensing something was going on, Mackenzie placed her hands on top of mine and said, "Let me see what you have going on over here." As much as I wanted her next to me, did it have to be at this very moment? Sliding my body along the kitchen island, a new escape route in motion, Mackenzie asked, "Are you ok Chris?"

Responding again, "I'm fine. Why do you ask?"

Sarcasm in her voice, "Maybe because you continue to distance yourself from me."

Looking at Mackenzie smirking and staring in my time of malfunction, I began to wonder if she had my body parts under some spell. She continued to stare down low, not once bringing her eyes up. Step by step, she returned in front of me, this time laughing hysterically. Tears pouring from the corner of each eye socket, Mackenzie commanded, "Chris move your hands."

Pretending I did not hear what she requested, I played dumb, "What did you say?"

Changing her tone, she said, this time with a more soothing delivery, "Will you please move your hands for me?" Per her request, I removed my hands slowly to my side. Squeezing my eyes closed, banking on a prayer that I was back to a normal state, I exposed the secret I could no longer hide.

"Wow," she said, eyes as large as watermelons.

Opening my eyes halfway, I looked down to find there

had been no change in appearance. Shaking my head, I said with my hands covering my face, "This is so embarrassing."

"For who," biting down on her lip. "I'm actually intrigued."

This woman was full of surprises. The things I thought would push her away had the reverse affect. In fact, instead of running for the door, she began washing my dishes. Excusing myself into the bedroom, I took a moment to have an intervention with my mini me down below.

Walking back and forth along my carpet, I cradled my penis assuming that in Mackenzie's absence, it would go back down. My ears zooming in on footsteps fast in speed, loud in tone, I took a quick peak out into the hallway, no longer a visible sight of Mackenzie. It appeared that I had finally scared Mackenzie off and if I were her, I'd probably leave too. Not only had I kissed her without permission or even a heads up, but I had exposed an erection after promising to be a gentleman. The night ruined by yours truly, I sat on my bed feeling completely defeated. The thought did cross my mind to chase after her, but by the time I made it out the door, she'd probably be gone and maybe it was for the best. My back pressed against the mattress, eyes staring at my ceiling, I sat lonely, feeling sorry for myself and then, out of nowhere, the sound of a saxophone hummed through the speakers of my home.

The sound of footsteps picked back up, this time the sound was accompanied by a strut as though this person had an agenda, a mission to seek out. Steps no longer visible as if they had come to a halting red light instead, they were replaced with a knock at my bedroom door.

Hoping Mackenzie was at the door, nervous that she was not as I was under the impression that she left, I opened the door with caution and there she was. In my head I thought, THANK GOD.

Welcoming herself into my room, mouthing not a single word, Mackenzie made herself comfortable on my bed. Joining with the intention of keeping my distance, I instead tripped over my own two feet and on top of Mackenzie I landed. Don't get me wrong, there were so many things that I wanted to do to Mackenzie's body and many men in my position would have seen their thoughts through, but I could not allow myself to go there. I respected her way too much to go any faster than she wanted. Removing myself from Mackenzie's personal space, she asked, "Chris, are you not attracted to me?"

"Baby, I am more than attracted to you," I assured her while gently rubbing her back.

Displaying a tone of doubt, Mackenzie disputed my claim, "I mean, the mood is right and all night you've either run away from me or given me the cold shoulder." Torn between what I wanted to do and what I should do, I reassured her, "You have no idea all the things I'd like to do to you."

Straddling her leg over mine, Mackenzie was on top of me with her arms crossed around my neck. Kissing each side of my face, nibbling down on my ear lobe, she had me. No longer could I fight any urge that I had been able to contain until now.

Taking it upon herself to remove my shirt over my head, she threw it on the side of the bed, placed her hair behind her ears and greeted my chest with a thousand kisses that I gladly welcomed.

Her kisses stopped completely, Mackenzie lifted from the bed, towards my bedroom door.

Dimming the lights, Mackenzie walked out into the hallway where she began to change the station on the satellite radio. Resting my back on the headboard of my bed, I watched as Mackenzie's leg resurfaced in the corner of my eye, the rest of her body cued by Silks, Meeting in My Bedroom. Her body moved to each and every note of the song as if she choreographed the entire dance bringing your boy back to the high school dances in the school gym, my hormones all over the damn place.

Thinking she'd just thrown a prop in my direction, I removed the object from my face to find Mackenzie topless, the prop in my hand, her shirt. Breaking into the splits, her backside facing me, I began to reach for my wallet, recalling that I had several one-dollar bills inside. Not sure if she'd take offense to my display of excitement throwing money her way, I left my wallet alone further enjoying the performance.

Never did I imagine the night going this way. The further into the song, the more articles of clothing she was without. Her belt slowly left her hips, removed from each loop that surround her waist. Her hands, she used to caress her inner thighs as she made her way towards the front zipper of her pants.

Slowly unbuttoning her pants, Mackenzie appeared in front of me where she placed her hands on her hips while looking down, signaling I grab hold of her zipper.

Responding to her cue, I brought my body to the edge of the bed where I placed each hand on both sides of her waist and began kissing up and down her stomach as she continued to dance, this time, using her hands to rub my head in slow motion. Pulling away, Mackenzie turned her body around, sat on my lap, and began grinding on me. Her body too enticing to just stare, I turned her back around, lifted her half naked body from the ground, and gently laid her down onto my mattress.

My respect for Mackenzie wouldn't allow me to go any further without asking, "Are you sure we aren't going too far? I don't want you to do anything you're uncomfortable with." Paused for a moment of silence, Mackenzie shifted her head in the opposite direction of mine where she appeared to be contemplating whether or not we should continue. If she wanted to stop, I had no problem respecting her wishes.

Mackenzie was too special to ruin what we had going.

Our eyes met again, she grabbed my face and with a look of both passion and certainty, confirmed, "All I want is you Chris."

And there it was! Mackenzie was single, I was single, and together we made sense. Her moans validated the pleasure felt which I shouted a few myself. It wouldn't surprise me if I woke up to a notice of disturbance nailed to my front door from my neighbors. Of course, I wanted their respect seeing as though we lived in the same building, but so much more, I wanted Mackenzie to experience a magical night and if that meant I would have to answer to the complaint from my neighbors, I was willing to take that risk.

After three hours of non-stop sex, in my arms she had fallen asleep.

Wanting to freeze the image of Mackenzie resting peacefully in my arms, I looked at her and wondered if she was the missing piece to my almost perfect life. Placing a kiss to her forehead, I rested my head near hers and I too fell fast asleep.

THE NEXT MORNING

The sunlight, aiming directly into my eyes, I awoke to find myself completely stretched out on the bed. Waking up, having experienced the most amazing, intimate dream that Mackenzie had come over and that we had made love, I just didn't want to wake from such a beautiful fairytale.

Sitting up from the bed, I rubbed my eyes, looked down to find I was without boxers. Standing upright, I sifted through my sheets in search of the boxers I thought I'd had on before falling asleep. Two steps to my right, a piece of material brushed against my foot which I thought at first, the missing boxers that had gotten tangled in my covers, instead I found numerous articles of female clothing which I now found myself puzzled.

Scratching my head, I sat back down on the bed, attempting to put the pieces together of last night which may not have been a dream after all. Commotion coming from outside my bedroom, I became more and more confused. Underwear nowhere in sight, I grabbed a pair of shorts which also lay on my floor and walked into the hallway unsure of who or what was in my home. My stride hesitant out the room, an aroma filled the air, leading me into the kitchen. It reminded me of my mother's cooking, but surely she wasn't here in my home, was she? How would she have gotten in?

A moment of clarity stepping into my kitchen and it all made sense. What I thought a dream; reality. The clothing that decorated the floor surrounding my bed was that of Mackenzie who stood half naked in my kitchen making breakfast. Not only was she cooking, but cleaning out the cabinets I had attempted to hide remnants of my messy lifestyle. All this, with only her bra and panties on.

This image, I could certainly get used to.

Turning on my charm, I snuck up behind her, moved her silky hair to the left side of her neck and kissed her good morning. Not startled at all that I walked up behind her, Mackenzie had a fork full of food prepared for me to try as if this were a daily ritual the two of us were accustomed. Opening wide, I took three bites and man, I was in a trance. Tied with my mother, her food was delicious and comforting.

Forcing out of her hand, the spatula, I scooped her round cakes into my hands, lifted her sexy body on top of the counter, and kissed her lips not once, not twice, but three times as a proper good morning greeting. Holding the top of my head, arching it forward, Mackenzie kissed the center of my head and said, "Good morning sleepy head."

Resting on top of her black lace bra which held her DD sized breasts that were most appetizing, "Good morning beautiful. What are you up to in here?" Looking around the kitchen, "Well I thought I would clean your messy kitchen and make you a little thank you breakfast before I left for work."

"Keep it up and I might keep you around," I said, thinking I could get used to her being here.

Smiling confidently, "I hope you do."

"Thank you, Mackenzie," I said, kissing her soft lips yet again.

Hopping off the counter, she finished wiping down the kitchen, "You are very welcome. I do want to clarify something Chris." Rinsing the sponge, she turned and said, "To set the record straight, I do not make it a habit of sleeping with someone so suddenly. I don't know what came over me last night."

"Sure you don't," making a small joke Mackenzie's facial expression showed she did not find humorous.

"I'm just kidding babe," blowing a kiss in her direction as a peace offering.

"You make me feel so alive and free," she said.

I did not want to see her go, but she had to hit the road for work. In fact, we both had to get to work which I was already late. Into my room she gathered her clothes and as much as I didn't want to see her leave, I had to let her go, reminding myself it was only temporary. Poking my lip out, saddened that she was preparing to walk out of my front door, I bared witness to the brightest most beautiful smile which shifted my bitterness.

Holding each other close for a short moment with an exchange of a kiss, down the hall I watched Mackenzie travel before her image vanished completely and out of my sight she was no longer. Late for work, without any urgency, my footsteps were light and slow to speed. I missed her already and longed for the next time I would see her again.

I kept going back to the weeks that continued to pass by, investigating whether or not she was taken before making my move and I realized that had I continued down the road of fear, I would remain in a state of WHAT IF and into someone else's hands she would be. Mackenzie didn't know it yet, but she was going to be mine. Nothing or no one was going to get in the way.

CHAPTER ELEVEN

Please Say Yes

Officially dating for the past six months, I wanted to prove how serious and committed I was, offering Mackenzie complete access to my home. I cleared half of the walk-in closet, had a key made for her to enter and exit as she pleased, even gave her the passcode to my phone which she never asked and certainly didn't have to. Mackenzie was the only woman in my life and whatever I had to do to prove this, I was prepared to step up to the plate.

Between Mackenzie being a traveling nurse and having to rush across town to get ready for work, I thought it much more convenient to get dressed here, leaving necessary essentials from her home over to mine which she happily accepted the invitation.

Missing her presence while away, I at least had her personal belongings near as a gentle reminder that she would soon return; her trips anywhere from three days to two weeks apart. Those week-long trips often left a lingering sense of loneliness, but oh, when she returned, you better believe she let a brotha know that she missed him just as much as I missed her.

Mom and dad now knew of Mackenzie, specific details left out of course. No way, no how was I going to share with them that she frequented my home whenever in town and I sure as hell wasn't going to let my mother catch wind of our sex life which was non-stop. Wanting to put a face with a name I spoke of so much, mom and dad invited both Mackenzie and I home for a weekend stay.

Dad expressing interest to meet Mackenzie also, it was mom's urgent desire that forced me to give her a specific date and time which we would arrive. Our weekly call pattern no longer routine, mother became curious, referencing Mackenzie as "that girl" wanting to know what spell she had me under.

The more I thought about moms concerns and reservations, Mackenzie did indirectly impact my lack of communication with my mother. You see, with her, I forgot that the outside world existed. She had my undivided attention and when apart, I daydreamed for the day she would return. Uncertain as to how she would respond, I invited Mackenzie to join me on the road for a weekend trip to visit my parents which she happily agreed to accompany me.

EN ROUTE

Conducting a Q & A session, Mackenzie wanted me to weigh in on how I thought the visit would go and if in fact she was the kind of girl my parents would expect for me to bring home. "Do you think your mom and dad will like me," she asked rather timid.

Cuffing her chin, I assured, "Baby, my family is going to love you. Stop worrying so much."

"I know how moms can be. No one can ever be good enough for their baby boys," she said unconvinced that my mother would in fact like her.

Reaching for her hand as she sat in the passenger seat, paranoid about this visit, "Baby, you'll be fine. I don't just take anyone to meet my parents. You are very special to me and it's time they know it too. Besides, I have something that I want to share with each of you." Little did Mackenzie know, I was going to kill two birds with one stone while on this trip. A surprise prepared that would further strengthen all that we were thus far.

Terror ringing from her vocals, she held on to my arm, her fingers trembling and asked, "Is everything ok? Are we ok Chris?"

Fighting the urge to reveal my secret, I vowed to her, "When the time is right, I will share the news and yes baby, we are just fine."

Why was I surprised to find mother peeking out of the blinds as I had messaged her via text that we were thirty minutes away. As if she had her own personal timer that she sat, she appeared at the exact moment that Mackenzie and I pulled into the driveway. The front door wide open before I even placed the car in park.

My forehead planted firmly on the steering wheel, I held my hand towards the front windshield and introduced the appearance of my mother to Mackenzie. "I present to you, my mother." As any real man would do, I ran to the front passenger side door where I escorted my lady love out of the car, her nerves displayed in the form of goosebumps on her arms.

Resting her hand in mine, together we walked up the driveway, Mackenzie preparing her first introduction, myself a reintroduction with my parents.

Praying a smooth first impression between all parties, we stood face to face with my mother, the queen of opinion.

With a promise not to leave her side, I stood right by Mackenzie as my mother stood, staring at us both with neither a happy nor disappointing facial expression. Still and silent which was anything like her, my mother appeared to be taking the atmosphere, an opinion not yet formed. As I explained to Mackenzie, I did not make it a habit bringing girls home to my parents.

My charm, which had never failed me before, I used to

break the thick layer of ice surrounding us along with the awkward silence. "Hey mom. You look beautiful as always."

Turning into mush, my mom's blank stare reshaped into a bright smile. Her arms outstretched, she commanded, "Come here and give your mother a hug." Two steps forward, one arm wrapped around my mother, the other gripped tightly, circulation almost lost, the captive, Mackenzie who had yet to release her anxiety.

Wanting not to leave my lady out, I broke free of the hand now numb and nudged her forward so that she too could join in conversation with my mother. Both of my ladies before me, I grabbed hold of their hands, held them close and introduced my beautiful lady to my beautiful mother. "Mom, I have someone I would like for you to meet."

Barely a tip toe forward, "This is my girlfriend Mackenzie. Mackenzie this is my mother Mrs. Harris."

Breaking free from my hand, my mother stood toe to toe with Mackenzie and I couldn't lie nor deny the fear that she was about to cause a scene due to the assumption that Mackenzie was keeping me away. My eyes shut completely, I began to pray wanting not to tip off to Mackenzie that I was also fearful of mother's behavior.

A release of laughter from my mother, my eyes reopened wide to find anything, but an altercation. My mother instead, held on to Mackenzie's arms as I still had one of her hands and with an open heart, "You must be the one who stole my son's heart. We've heard so much about you. It is so nice to finally meet."

Two thumbs in the air, mom released a verbal approval, "She is stunning Chris. You remind me of myself at your age Mackenzie." Mackenzie took one look at me, releasing her hand from the fold of mine and stood next to my mother, no longer afraid.

"That is so kind of you Mrs. Harris," she replied to my mother's comment. Placing her hands on top of my mothers, more comfortable now, Mackenzie began touring the exterior of the home, returning my mother's compliment with one of her very own. "You have a lovely home Mrs. Harris."

Exiting from the circle of communication, Mackenzie strolled over towards my mother's flowerbed where she leaned forward, taking in the fragrance of each petal. Looking over in our direction, Mackenzie politely excused herself and asked, "Mrs. Harris are these pink carnations?"

My existence no longer a thought, my mother too excited, leaving me on the porch by myself. Leaning forward along with Mackenzie, my mother turned and said, "A woman who knows flowers. Oh, she's a keeper alright."

With a wave of my mother's hand, "Leave us alone Chris, we have a garden to discuss. Go say hello to your father."

Using my keen psychological sense, I zoomed in close for any hesitation Mackenzie may have been attempting to send in a way that only I was able to decode.

The two disappearing on the side of the house, I had to look no further and in the house, I searched for dad.

Listening for signs of my father, I walked down the hall, startled by an angry shout, "What the hell," and I knew exactly where he was.

In the den I entered to find my father watching the ball game, his team obviously losing.

If I learned anything about my father, it was to never, ever, ever, interrupt him while he was watching sports. That act could cause serious injury. Stepping past him, I silently tapped his leg and said, "What's up pops," refraining from any further conversation until the game was over. His eyes glued to the television, he responded, "Hey Chris," as if I had never left for New York and had been home the entire time.

Next to his recliner chair, I made certain to sit quiet as a church mouse making no sudden moves. The opposing team making a three-point shot at the buzzer and my dad was pissed, shouting so loud at the television that his beer fell onto the floor, rolling next to my shoe. Thankfully the can had not been opened.

"Hand me that Chris," my father asked, completing a double take.

"CHRIS," he shouted in excitement, "Is that you son?"

The game over, dad was finally able to give me his undivided attention having clearly missed the first greeting I gave. Playing along as if I'd just entered the room, "Hey dad!" Smacking the side of my shoulder, he searched around and asked, "You doing ok son? Where's that pretty lady?"

"Hanging out with mom in the garden," I responded, butterflies fluttering at even the reference of Mackenzie.

Sitting back, propping his seat up with the side lever, "Everything going well down in New York? We haven't heard from you much."

I came to town with all good news to report with an additional trick up my sleeve which I'd pitch to dad later in the day, "I know dad. I've been extremely busy with work," I said, trying hard to play off what really had my mind, body and soul occupied. "The kids would love to meet you." A pleased look on his face, not one to smile often, dad leaned in with a compliment, "You look good son. Have you been working out?"

"Well, kind of," depending on what he meant by working out. Had I stepped foot inside a physical gym, no. Had I been introduced to yoga, aerobics, Pilates with Mackenzie in the bedroom, but of course.

Dad, no fool at all, caught my subliminal response. "Chris? Is it safe to assume that you have been using the package I sent you six months ago?"

Yes and no, both honest answers to his very direct question. What started out as the practice of safe sex, quickly transitioned to occasional practice and after a month or so, no practice at all. It was something about being inside of her that placed me in a trance, unable to think clearly. She was unbothered by the absence of condoms, my forgetfulness to pull out, and the reality of what could occur if we continued on this path we had grown so familiar.

Equal blame shared as we both played a role in the unprotected passion that consumed our souls and we did not care. Mackenzie was happy, I was happy and we needed no outside approval to continue down a road of bliss. The opportunity passed to respond to dad's assumption, mom and Mackenzie both appeared in the room. Resting her hands on my father's shoulders, my mother introduced my father to my lady. "Mackenzie, this is Chris's father, Mr. Harris."

Standing from the chair, both my father and Mackenzie shook hands. Nodding his head up and down, staring back at me, "Great job Chris!" Facing Mackenzie again, "It is very nice to meet you little lady."

Mother standing front and center of the room, delivered news that even I didn't believe knowing who my mother was. "Our dear Mackenzie has just offered to make tonight's dinner which I can't wait to try."

Mom was either sick in the head or had fallen for Mackenzie just as fast as I did. To allow another set of hands to prepare our family meal was unheard of. I mean, mother was relinquishing all rights to the kitchen, handing them off to a total stranger she'd only heard of and known for less than an hour. Quite the work load, I did not want Mackenzie overwhelmed or feeling as though she had to go the extra mile to impress my parents, "You don't have to do that honey."

"You know how to cook Mackenzie," my dad asked in seriousness. With laughter, Mackenzie responded, "Yes sir, I do." Leaping from his recliner, a man who loved to eat and try new things, wrapped his arms around both my lady and his, "Well in that case, let my wife and I show you the kitchen because she has been slacking since Chris left."

Offended by his comment, mom offered a suggestion that instantly silenced my father, "You said you would like to sleep on the couch tonight, did I hear correct?"

No response at all, dad stepped back into the distance where he spoke only when spoken to. My parents hadn't changed one bit since relocating and I wanted the same for Mackenzie and I. They may have gotten underneath each other's skin, but there was never any doubt that the love they had for one another was real.

Introducing Mackenzie to the contents in the kitchen cabinets, my mother apologized in advance, "I'm sorry I'm a bit unprepared. I haven't been to the store this week, but I'm positive that anything you need that we do not have here, my husband and Chris will be glad to run to the store," clearing her throat.

Examining each cabinet, Mackenzie passed me by, but not before displaying affection in front of my parents as she rubbed against my chest. The same charm I used on others, Mackenzie was learning to use on me as if she even had to try. Requesting only a few small items from the store, we parted ways, but not before placing a kiss on her soft, delicate lips, "I got you babe." Lost in a moment of passion, our kiss held still, mom had no problem interjecting, "Alright you two."

Collecting a pen and pad of paper from a nearby drawer, mom stood in between Mackenzie and I as if she could regulate our desire to be near one another. Keeping Mackenzie completely occupied, "You just write down what you need, and the men will go and get it," mom spoke, giving me the not so pleasant side eye.

Folding the detailed list of ingredients in half, mom slapped them across my father's chest who remained silenced in the corner as if he were a small boy in time-out. Sensing an argument preparing to erupt, I grabbed hold of dad and assisted him directly towards the front door and out of the line of fire. Besides, this gave me time to discuss with dad, my little plan that he could assist with.

Perturbed he was, I could not help, but find humor in his childish pout.

Offering to chauffeur dad for a change, this would allow him time to clear his mind and me to express what was on mine. Laying the cards on the table, I held nothing back, and allowed my heart to flow into my dad's ears. "Dad, I have never cared for any one the way that I care for Mackenzie. She is intelligent, beautiful, makes me laugh, and with her, I feel like nothing can go wrong in my life."

"Sounds like you may be in love son. Have you shared these feelings with her," dad asked.

There was absolutely no confusion about what this was with Mackenzie. I wasn't in lust nor strong like, I loved this woman and I wanted to clarify that with my father first. "I am beyond in love dad which is why I need your help."

"Why is that son," his head turned.

Keeping my eyes on the road, I pointed to the right of me, giving my father specific directions, "Would you reach in the center console and grab the white bag for me?"

Following my direction, he removed the white bag from the console and retrieved a bright red box which he held in his hand. Asking my permission, he opened the box wide, his first impression I could not make out, focused on the road ahead and not just the driving road, the road that involved Mackenzie and I as one if she would have me.

"Wow, this is nice son. Are you sure you're ready for this?"

Each opportunity I had to display the desire in my eyes to my father, I took advantage. "I want to make her my wife. I know that we have only been together for six months, but dad, I cannot imagine living a second without her. I'd be crazy if I allowed fear to block my blessing."

My father, never one to judge, rather educate and voice his thoughts based on personal experience, spoke from the perspective of a married man which I valued.

"I believe what you are telling me son, but I want you to know that marriage is forever. You cannot turn it on and off just because you two disagree or have an argument. It takes commitment, much patience, and faith in God to withstand both the good and bad. You're on a high now, but there will come a time when she gets on your last nerve and you will question whether to stay, stray, or go. The devil has his way of introducing temptation at the right moment and you're going to have to turn a blind eye. You will have to learn to stick it out for better or worse and worse is one thing you cannot avoid," he spoke.

Stopped at a red light, the two of us shared a moment, my father pouring knowledge into my soul. "The moment you say I Do, there will be no more Chris, instead, Mr. & Mrs. Harris as a unit. Can you handle that?"

If he didn't hear me the first time, I was going to make him hear me now. My chest out, head high, with confidence, I responded, "I was ready the day I met her dad."

"Well then, congratulations son."

Not much on the list, we were in and out of the store in no time in route of our ladies. I made sure to conceal the box I carried from the car to my parents' house wanting to raise no suspicion or give my surprise away.

Catching dad before he entered the house, I pleaded, "Hey dad." Stopped in his tracks, carrying the two bags of groceries, "Yes son?"

"Please don't say anything, not even to mom," I begged.

I had no intentions of keeping this news away from my mother, but she could not hold water and I knew that if I told her now, this wouldn't come as a surprise to Mackenzie.

I decided to wait until after dinner before asking the woman I loved to marry me, this way I could calm my nerves and think of the right words to say. My only fear is that she would say no which I'm not sure my heart could handle such a response. Time racing, dinner was prepared and served in under two hours which seemed like two minutes to me. Joining as one, we came together in the dining room where Mackenzie even set the dinner table.

My queen had prepared crusted salmon sprinkled with lemon juice and parsley, rice pilaf, perfectly tenderized asparagus, and for dessert, a moist red velvet cake with such attention to detail that it belonged in a magazine. Over and over in my head, I thought of how I would make my proposal as I only had one chance to do this right. Appetite completely gone thanks to my overreacting nerves, I sat back and watched as Mackenzie and my mother shared a few laughs. She was a perfect fit for my family and most importantly; my life.

After consuming seconds, my dad thirds, we had concluded dinner in which everyone was stuffed. Mackenzie, being the sweetheart she was, walked around collecting everyone's plates from the dining room table. In constant motion, I waited for the right moment to stop her, but the fear in me continued to postpone what only dad was familiar with.

Sensing my nervousness which wasn't hard to do as I had already broken a sweat, dad stepped in to open the floor.

"Chris, wasn't there something you wanted to share with us," nodding his head, cheering me on. Becoming hysterical, mom dropped her utensils onto her plate which sparked the most irritating sound to ring through our ears, "Chris, what is it son?"

Rising from my seat, I walked over to the love of my life where I stood behind her chair, resting my hand on her shoulders as I spoke. "Mom, dad, Mackenzie, I would like to take a moment to share something with each of you."

Directing everyone into the living room for a more relaxed setting, I waited for Mackenzie to finish clearing the table as she felt obligated seeing she was the one to prepare dinner. Everyone in the room, the time had come and there was no turning back. Mom sat on the edge of her seat, Mackenzie held a confused look as we had no secrets between us, while dad remained relaxed, aware of my plans.

Deep breath in and out, I began to choke as I uttered, "Mom and dad, I am in love with this woman," pointing at Mackenzie who had been exposed to this confession for the very first time.

Befitting that she sat on the love seat which welcomed two persons, I invited myself to join her where I took her hand into mine to further my thoughts.

Lifting her hand into the air, I placed a lasting kiss on her palm before continuing. "I love everything about you. You make me feel whole and when you're not around, I'm empty inside. From the moment I met you, I knew that there was something special. Mackenzie the risk of losing you is one I am not willing to take, ever."

Mackenzie and my mother brought to tears, I pondered how to introduce the ring and proposal that I was praying she would accept. Lifting from my seat, I pretended that I pulled a muscle in my leg, leaning over to soothe it. "Ouch, my leg. I think I just pulled a muscle." The false pain that I exhibited, brought both my mother and Mackenzie out of their seats in efforts to check my well-being. This right here, the perfect opportunity to remove the ring from my back pocket, both ladies standing in front of me.

Looking back at dad one final time, receiving the all clear nod, I was getting ready to kneel down and when I returned I'd either be an engaged man or heartbroken. Using Mackenzie's hand as leverage, I got down on one knee, looked up above at the most beautiful angel, and asked the most important question of my life before my loved ones, "Mackenzie, I have one question for you." Pulling the box from my back pocket, displaying the ring that sparkled through the entire room, "WILL YOU MARRY ME?"

Dad remained seated smiling from ear to ear, mom had run to the nearest phone telling everyone the news which made the stakes even higher as I had yet to receive a yes or no response.

Mackenzie, silent, tears running down her cheeks, overcome by emotion that hindered a response.

Lifting from the ground, I consoled her using one hand to wipe the tears away, the other to soothe her back. Arching her chin up, I kissed her damp lips, the tears running past, and asked, "Will you make me the happiest man on earth and be my wife?" Her arms wrapped behind my neck, face resting on my shoulder, she whispered, "Chris, I would love nothing more than to marry you."

"So is that a YES," I asked, seeking confirmation.

"YES!!!!!"

My father springing from his chair, shouted yes as if he were in the bleachers of a basketball game, his team standing in the lead. Mother, yet to get off the phone, screamed from the kitchen, "Congratulations you two. We can't wait to meet your family Mackenzie." The atmosphere high in excitement all except Mackenzie whose mood shifted the moment my mother mentioned "family." The entire time we had been together, Mackenzie spoke little about her family or maybe I spoke too much of mine. Whatever the case, out of all the years I'd studied psychology, never had I seen the expression Mackenzie displayed on anyone who had just accepted a wedding proposal.

Emotions high, mom planning the wedding we had yet to set a date, dad discussing whether or not our future children would call him Paw Paw or Pops, Mackenzie the only party staring off into the distance, exempt from the happiness that filled the room.

I wasn't sure what was going on through Mackenzie's head, but make no mistake, I was going to make it my mission to find out.

CHAPTER TWELVE

Mistaken Identity

Exchanging goodbyes, both Mackenzie and I had to return back to work.

My mother, yet to come off of her pedestal of excitement, approached Mackenzie, requesting, "You take care of my son now daughter-in-law." Staring off into the distance again, Mackenzie responded, "I sure will Mrs. Harris," her voice barely heard.

Back inside the house my parents went, Mackenzie and I headed towards the car. I must have waited at least five minutes on Mackenzie who continued to drag her feet from the front porch to the front of the car. I could see now that this was going to be an interesting drive home. Barely able to keep my eyes on the road, my fiancé' quiet without the exchange of two words since saying, "yes," to my proposal.

Twisting her ring left and right up and down, one could only assume she was having second thoughts about getting married. Lord knows I did not want to pick a fight, but I needed her to tell me what was going through her mind so that we could come to some understanding.

Placing my right hand on her lap, I caressed her thigh and asked, "Are you ok baby?"

Removing her fingers from her ring she continued to fidget with, she brushed my hand away and shouted, highly irritated, "Yes, why wouldn't I be fine?"

Her emotions were all over the place and here I was simply trying to offer support. My dad did tell me there would be rough times ahead, but never did I image they would appear the moment we became engaged. Responding to her question, "After the proposal you shut down completely. My mom mentioned meeting your parents and you just froze. I've never seen you like this before. Now I'm watching you play with your ring as if you want to take it off. What's going on?"

Fearing that our relationship was in jeopardy, this the first time we experienced what could be a difference in opinion, I asked the Lord to guide my words.

Her tone now calm, "I'm fine Chris. I just wasn't expecting a proposal."

As long as we had been together, the passion and desire burned bright and now all of a sudden, she was caught off guard? Unlike other men, I was not a fan of playing house rather build a house. I did not want an *in and out* girlfriend any longer, but a wife to love, honor and protect; and all of a sudden, my proposal caught her off guard? What did she think we were leading up to after all this time?

Confused by her response, "I don't understand how asking you to marry me caught you off guard. If anything, I thought you'd be ecstatic. I love you and you love me, right? It's only natural for two people who love each other, who spend a decent amount of time as one, who've experienced the company of one another's parents which I'll soon meet yours, to join together as one; am I right?"

Her lips sealed shut, leaving me frustrated without any words left to say.

"Chris, I don't want to talk about it. Just let it go," she yelled. Clearly I had spent this morning with Mackenzie's evil twin because this woman here, I had never met before. This woman had my heart and we had come way too far to allow secrets to stand in our path.

"Mackenzie you're going to have to tell me something babe because the way you're acting makes it seem like you don't want to get married and if that's the case, I need to know."

"I'm fine," she responded in a dismissive tone.

She may have thought that response was going to suffice, but it didn't, not with me.

My right signal on, I awaited two cars to pass before changing lanes, getting off at the nearest rest stop. I needed no distraction to have an adult conversation with Mackenzie. We were going to settle these underlying issues here and now. Eliminating even the sound of the engine, I took the keys out of the ignition. Seatbelt off, I turned directly towards Mackenzie who sat quiet as she had been the last twenty-four hours. Pleading with her, I asked, "What is it?"

Turning away from me, sticking to the same response she now had on replay, "I said nothing Chris. Just leave it alone." Making my voice loud, my words very clear, "If we plan to create a future with one another, secrets are one thing I will not tolerate. You are soon to be my wife and whatever is bothering you, affects the both of us so again, what's wrong?"

Leaning her head against the glass of the passenger side window, I could hear a faint sniff as she tried to hide the tears she began to shed. Wondering if I had been too harsh with my tone, I placed my worry aside to step in and console my soon to be wife who was obviously battling something inside.

Pulling her towards my chest, I held her close as she broke down. Afraid to let go, underneath my chin I could hear muffled words that were in deep competition with her shortness of breath. "I look at the relationship you have with your mother and it's one I'll never be able to share with my own. She abandoned me as a little girl and it has just been myself and my father ever since. I always thought she would come looking for me and she never did. When your mom mentioned my family, I realized that I didn't have one to introduce. How could I ruin the moment by saying that?"

Our eyes, staring deep into the other, "Of course I'm excited to become your wife, but a wedding is an experience you share with your mother. I won't have her around to watch me try on my dress or tell me that I look beautiful."

Her head hanging low, "It just hurts so bad."

Pulling her away from my chest, using my thumbs to remove the tears from her eyes, I arched her chin, kissed her lips for comfort, and asked, "Why didn't you tell me this before baby?" Not a secret between us, I was taken back that I was not made aware of this privy information. She even knew about Mike and yet such pain she kept inside, she kept from me. Why?

"I just told you that it's embarrassing. How would you feel if your mother left you; never wanting you in the first place?

My father has been my rock and he was all that I had until I met you. You filled a void of loneliness that I found nearly impossible to cope. For a moment in my life, I had forgotten her existence as she had no intentions of seeking mine."

As much as I did not want to see her in any form of pain, I found this information extremely important which I needed to know. This internal pain she kept bottled inside had the potential of interfering in our own marriage and at least now, I knew what to look for. It hurt me deeply to learn that anyone would turn their back on such an amazing woman, but it wasn't Mackenzie's fault that her mom missed out on the opportunity to get to know a gem. This was her mother's own loss and not one Mackenzie should suffer. I wanted to love her so much more so that she would never ever spend another day yearning for the love of a person too cowardly to give love in return.

Just as Mackenzie made me lose focus of the outside

world as we knew it, I was glad that I could do the same for her. This confirmed the fact that we were meant to be. We took the pain from one another, wrapped it away tightly in a gift box, and sat on it with our undying love for each other.

"Baby," calling for her attention.

"Please don't ever feel that you cannot confide in me. No matter how bad it hurts, if you think it may cause further pain, I want to be there to eliminate any fear, doubt, or worry that consumes. You are my queen. I will never do anything to make you feel that you cannot trust me and I know you'd do the same for me." I had to assure Mackenzie that I would never hurt her and that I was totally committed to our love, forever. Nothing was going to tear us apart, especially if I had anything to do with it.

Although broken in certain areas of her life, these battles, I was willing to fight with her and not against her and I believed that I had proved my position. We made it safely back to New York, so glad we were able to work through our first rough patch.

Welcoming our return home with a magical kiss, Mackenzie had to head off on yet another business trip. Thankfully, this one had the time frame of only three days which I think I was strong enough to handle. She promised to return in time for the Greater Faith annual picnic which was a well-known annual event people traveled far distances to attend. This event, hosted by the Pastoral Committee, allowed churches from other states the opportunity to unite together for great fellowship, worship, and good ole home cooking.

You never knew who you would run into at these events. I was told by one of the elders that last year's picnic brought T.D. Jakes, Maurette Brown Clark, Fred Hammond, just to name a few. Who I would come in contact, I was not sure, but could not wait.

THE PICNIC

It was the morning of the picnic and who was resting beautifully in my arms, Mackenzie, who had decided to spend the night so that we could travel together as one to the event. She was my real life sleeping beauty and knowing that I was one step closer towards giving her my last name was an indescribable feeling.

She looked so adorable in her tennis skirt and athletic top. My own little Serena Williams.

Going by rumor only of what this event looked like, I was certainly glad that I came. The commentators did not do this picnic justice. Churches from all over gathered with the Greater Faith family. I mean if you didn't hold your loved ones close, you were likely to lose them in the crowd. Taking in the scenery, it was hard to decide where to make our presence known first.

Would we start at the food line which extended for miles and miles? If the food taste as great as it smelled, it was going to go down in my stomach, but after the line had gone down a bit. Would we make our rounds to the many booths that circled the park? Some booths filled with informative health information, others pertaining to owning your own business, while many others, entrepreneurs marketing products they wished to sell.

My lady in my arms rather quiet, I figured she was taking it all in like I had been doing the past ten minutes, wanting not to assume; however, I asked with her hand cuffed in my arm, "Are you ok my love?" Removing her hand from my arm, grabbing hold of her stomach, she crouched down, "I woke up with lower abdominal pain. I think I just need to eat something."

That response gave the exact location of our first stop, food line. I was going to get myself and my baby a plate to eat.

I sure hoped this made her feel better because she looked flushed and I really wanted her to have a great time.

Walking over to an unoccupied picnic table, I guided Mackenzie down on the bench and went and stood in line for the both of us so that she could rest herself until I returned. "Sit tight while I fix your plate. I'll grab you a water too."

The line moving rather fast, halted by a brief moment of chaos. While in line, I had witnessed two fights among members upset at either the fact that they felt the lines were taking too long, the portions served were too small, and/or the person in front cut the line. I was tickled that those much older than myself were behaving in such an unpleasant manner, but hey, who was I to judge.

Moving down the assembly line of food, I thanked the volunteer servers, a few familiar faces, exiting the line grabbing two cold bottles of water before returning to my honey.

A few short feet away, I witnessed a man whom I did not recognize, approach Mackenzie while she rest on the bench. One foot leaning on the bench, elbow on top of his knee, I could tell he had either become comfortable in conversation as he possibly knew Mackenzie or was laying on similar skills as I had, only difference; I was one step ahead and about to return and break the bad news.

Mackenzie and I had a strong foundation and I was not at all worried about any man stealing my woman. I was confident in myself as a man, but I knew that she wasn't feeling well and if this man was here to put what moves he thought he had, on her, although flattered myself at his courage, this was not the time. More than likely a visitor walking around, getting to know everyone, I did not fret over small talk. In fact, I was happy to join right in.

On the opposite side of both, I sat Mackenzie's plate down in front of her whose appearance had only worsened from the time I left to my return. "Why don't you try to eat something baby," resting her head on her arms which laid crossed on the picnic table. Unbothered by my appearance or the fact that I just called my woman "baby," the man remained and our union of two now became a party of three.

Hard to eat with this gentleman staring at us both, I wiped my mouth and cordially offered my hand. "Good afternoon! My name is Chris and you are?" High in personality, the gentleman practically pulled me onto the other side of the table with his handshake, "What's up Chris? My name is Brandon. I was just catching up with my girl Lauren over here." Who was Lauren? The only woman I saw was Mackenzie.

"Lauren," I looked around and asked.

As if this mysterious Lauren had joined us in conversation, Brandon continued, "Yes, she and I go back to the blacktop in high school." Sitting down next to Mackenzie, a bit closer than either of us was comfortable, he wrapped his arm around her, "Girl you have not changed a bit. Still fine as hell."

Putting this nonsense to rest, I interjected, "Look Brandon, that's your name, right? You have her mistaken for someone else in your past. Her name is Mackenzie. We don't have a clue who this Lauren is you keep referencing."

"Mackenzie," he said, scratching his head in confusion. "Naw this is Lauren. I smoked weed back in the day, but I'd never forget a pretty face."

My baby's facial expression was enough signal for me to excuse this weed smoking, delusional Brandon from our table so that we could eat in peace. Pointing my finger at Mackenzie for all eyes to see, speaking in a slow manner so that his mind could keep up and process, "This is my fiancé and I am sure that her name is not Lauren."

Scratching his head again, he asked one final time,

batting his eyes together, "You really aren't Lauren?"

"No, my name is Mackenzie," speaking up for the first time which she did not have to as she had nothing to prove. This man had a case of mistaken identity and fortunate for him, Lauren was still out there somewhere she just wasn't my Mackenzie. Excusing himself from the picnic table, he walked away apologizing, "My fault yall. I swear you look like this girl I went to high school with who dated my bro back in the day."

As long as he got the hint and proceeded in the opposite direction, there were no hard feelings, his apology accepted. "You're good man. Good luck finding Lauren."

Relieved that he was finally gone, I sat next to my lady after a brief moment of separation and could not help, but to laugh at such an interesting ten minutes. "Well sweetheart, you must have a beautiful twin out there named Lauren."

Shrugging her shoulders, offering no words, it was painfully clear that even after consuming a few small bites of food, Mackenzie's state wasn't improving.

"You really don't look well babe," I said.

Her words slurred, body slouched forward, "I don't feel very well." As much as I wanted to enjoy a nice picnic with our church family, Mackenzie needed to get home out of the sun and experience some TLC by her man. Stepping away for a brief moment to find something to cover her food up, I watched as she fought to stand up only collapsing back down onto the bench. Running to her aid, I held her up as she painfully spoke, "I'm sorry. Are you sure you're not mad at me?"

What was there to be mad at? If my fiancé did not feel good, nothing else mattered, but getting her back to a state of good health.

"Mad about what? Don't be sorry. Doctor Daddy is here for you," I winked.

Whatever it took, I was going to nurse my baby back to health. Her face discolored, complete loss of balance as we trailed slow to the car, the scent of food which rest in her lap forced us to pull over to the side of the road where she threw up several times before I realized that was the trigger of her upset stomach.

Ironically, she was the nurse, used to aiding others back to health. This time, I would have to suit up in her place, waiting hand and foot until that beautiful smile resurfaced. Whatever had come over my baby, I prayed it was only temporary and nothing too serious.

CHAPTER THIRTEEN

It Can't Be Her

"Marcus. What up boy," shouted Brandon from across the room. Now this was the last guy on earth you would ever find working out in the gym unless he was after a female which would then explain his visit.

"Brandon. What in the world are you doing here? Denim jeans and a button down, really," I asked in disbelief knowing he was up to no good. Popping his collar, he attempted to make sense of a story that made no sense at all.

"You aint the only dude who's trying to get buff," flexing his bird of a chest.

"Don't let the shortness fool you dog, I'm liftin like four twenty every day." How ironic of him to use the numbers four and twenty which explained a lot coming from him.

Standing from the work out bench I occupied to catch my breath, I called his bluff, "Are you willing to put your money where your mouth is," holding my hand out, offering a seat positioned under a pair of weights. "You see, I don't get paid 'til the first," stuttering away as the lies vomited from his mouth. Patiently waiting to learn the details which led him here, I sat back on the bench and listened to this crazy cat.

"How you been man," asked Brandon. Responding in between each bench press, "Tired. I've been working crazy hours at the fire station. I feel like I don't get any sleep or time with my lady."

"How is Lauren doing? I aint seen her in a minute."

My heart warmed just thinking of my woman, "She's good. Right now, she is on a business trip, but she should be back tomorrow night." Grabbing my water which sat on the floor next to me, it felt good to catch up with Brandon. It wasn't often that I could vocalize my frustration working tedious hours, "Between her business trips and my hectic work schedule, we barely see one another."

Brandon stepping outside of his humorous behavior, asked, "You ever tried taking a few days off to go on vacation with her? Surely being a fireman has its perks. You don't have any time off to just get away?"

Staring off into the distance, if it were only that simple.

"I would love to, but it seems that when I'm off or even want to take a little time off, she's leaving for another trip. I know she works hard, but sometimes I wish she'd just take a break. I never wanted her to work in the first place, but telling her that turns into an argument which she begins to feel as though I'm trying to control her. I just don't want her to work when she does not have to. We have a good life, I make more than enough so that she doesn't have to lift a finger, but you know how some women are? They have to uphold this Miss. Independent mentality which I don't hold against her."

"Hell, I wish these chicken heads I chase would get off their asses and work. Most of them won't because they will lose their TANF, WIC, and/or stamps. Let that girl work bro," his humor resurfaced.

I never understood his choice in women nor did I try. Compared to Lauren, no one stood a chance. That was my baby and our relationship was solid.

"Why do you mess with women who have nothing going for themselves?

I mean, it's one thing to need assistance for a short

period of time, but that help is only meant to be temporary. Lauren and I weren't always in a good place financially which is why we both worked hard to get where we are today. Surely these women you mess with want better for their lives." Staring me down with a look of seriousness, "Bro. Do you know what dinner is like on the first of the month messing around with these chicken heads? I eats good you feel me. They be hittin up the meat department cooking up filet mignon, shrimps, and fish. I ain't given that up besides not everybody wants to settle down like you."

Shaking my head back and forth, hard to believe some of the words that came from Brandon's mouth, "You are something else." Making Lauren the topic of discussion for a second time, Brandon asked, "How often does Lauren go on her business trips?"

The type of job she had, the trips were sporadic. Sometimes she was gone a day, a week, two, sometimes even a whole month depending on the form of training.

"Pretty frequently. Man wait, why are you asking so many questions about my woman," I could not help, but wonder.

Disregarding my curiosity, he followed up with a request, "Let me see a picture of her." What was this fool up to and why did he all of a sudden seek so much interest in my woman?

"What makes you think that I have a picture of her lingering around?" Poking his lips out, his arms crossed together, "Every sprung man has a picture of his woman either in his wallet or chest pocket, close to the heart. You know y'all pretty boys like to brag. " How detailed he was on where a picture should be kept considering he didn't know the first thing about commitment, "You sound like you speak from experience yourself."

Unlocking his arms, he began patting himself down, on a desperate search to see Lauren.

"Yep. I keep a condom in the wallet," pounding his back pocket. "And the digits," slapping his chest with his palm, "shirt pocket."

Licking his lips, "I'm sprung off that," making a meow sound.

Holding a heart to heart with this deeply flawed individual who happened to be one of my crazier friends, "Are you ever going to settle down? I mean don't you want to start a family?" Looking at me as if I disrespected his mother, "Hell naw. Now pull it out or how about this; I'm going to turn around and you tell me when to look. That way, I won't be able to crack jokes on you."

I was guilty, but not ashamed. I did have a picture of Lauren. It was her picture that made her absence manageable.

Peeking in my direction, his fingers wide spread, a horrible attempt at not looking, "You are a fool man. I knew you had a picture now give it to me," snatching it out of my hand.

"Oh shit. I knew that was her," picture falling to the floor.

No this fool did not just drop my baby's photo. "Be careful man," I said, picking my baby's photo up off the ground.

Walking short distances back and forth in front of me, the most serious I'd ever seen, what he said next, news I just could not bring myself to believe. "Naw man. I don't know how to say this to you, but I saw her over the weekend and it did not look like she was conducting any business."

Not sure if it was his extracurricular activities speaking, I listened, no rush to take what he had to say as factual. "You saw her where?" Standing at attention, he told me how they came in contact. "I went to this church up in New York City."

It had to be the weed. This man knew he did not partake in any church function, ever. I knew him long enough to know that much. Stopping him before he spoke another word as he was clearly hallucinating, "First of all, I know you are lying because you don't step foot in anybody's church. You have always complained that the service is too long and the pastors pocket the collection money. So I know you did not sit in anyone's service."

Clarifying his story, he made a few adjustments, his depiction further confusing. "You are absolutely right. I do not sit in any money hungry sanctuary with everybody screaming and acting like their feet were just set on fire."

Needing further clarification, "So how did you see her?"

"I was actually at a church picnic with one of my honey dips and that is where I spotted her." My head out of sorts, still trying to picture Brandon having any direct contact with the structure of any CHURCH.

"I'm still trying to place you and God in the same sentence," I said, scratching my head. "You better recognize. There are hell of females in there. I am a sinner looking to be saved by the booty," he confessed, holding both hands up to the Lord who was probably preparing to strike him down using his name and the word booty in the same sentence.

"Are you sure it was not someone who looked like her? You know your memory isn't the best."

"I wasn't smoking in the church dog, that ain't holy," he assured. Squinting my eyes, trying to make sense of what he was saying to me, "Oh, but looking at booty as you say, is?"

Pounding his chest with his palm, "Look, you my boy and I will always keep it real with you. I saw her with another guy and she was not at work. The dude was rubbing all over her back and it did not appear that they were strangers towards one another. I even confronted her and apparently she is going by the name, Mackenzie."

By his own omission, he did have the wrong woman.

"You see there; it was not her. She said that her name was Mackenzie not Lauren," I began to feel better.

Snatching the picture out of my hand, smashing it into my face which almost caught him two to the chest, "Bro, you just showed me a picture. Unless she has a twin whom you've never met, this is the woman I saw. Your woman to be exact."

My thoughts all over the place, "Do you know the name of this church B?"

He was able to recall this entire meet and greet so he claims to have had, but now that I needed him most, his memory went shot. Unable to recall the name of the church or who put on this so-called picnic, I was going to have to do some investigating to get to the bottom of this story that would either prove fact or fiction.

"All I can say bro," thinking hard, "Greater Faith put the picnic together, but if in fact this was the church she was frequenting, I couldn't say for sure." Snatching my keys and gym bag off the ground, I thanked Brandon for his help, "Right on Brandon," and left out the building with one thought in my head; find my woman.

"Hey, where you going Marcus? I need you to spot me," I could hear Brandon plea as the weights rested against his chest, his own stupidity to blame. Spotting Brandon underneath a pair of weights bound to kill him was not my concern at the moment. He was on his own and I was in a zone.

CHAPTER FOURTEEN

Disbelief

Outside my bathroom door I stood, waiting on Mackenzie who promised to be ready in ten minutes. Thirty minutes passed and still, she remained tucked behind the bathroom door. Delivering a soft knock, I called out, "Mackenzie. Are you ready babe? We're going to be late for church."

Having yet to consult a physician, I became worried about Mackenzie. Her illness on again off again and still, we had no answers as to what was causing her much discomfort. She could hardly eat, let alone keep her head up due to exhaustion. My baby just wasn't the same and I was doing everything I could to hold her up as her man, but there was only so much that I could do.

Awaiting a response which proved silent from Mackenzie, I thought it best that we stay home from church to give my baby time to heal. "Hey Ken? Why don't we just stay in today," I suggested. One flush after another and the door, cracked open, gave visual of Mackenzie at the sink, swooshing water back and worth into her mouth, releasing it into the vanity sink.

Pointing her index finger in the air, her face repositioned near the toilet, she spoke with little energy, "No. No. We're not missing church. Just give me one more minute."

My poor baby. It tore me up seeing her this way knowing there was nothing I could do to ease the pain.

"I'm ready," she said, struggling to stand.

Mackenzie was anything, but ready and I had to be the voice of reason. I had to be the legs she could not stand on. "Honey, I really think you need to go and see someone. You can't go on like this."

"I know," holding on to her stomach.

Not quite sure she understood the severity here, I grabbed hold of her hand, explaining, "I'm serious. You can't eat a bite of food without throwing up. You sleep more than usual, and you keep holding on to these recurring stomach cramps. I'm worried about you."

Leaning into my shoulder, she said, "Honey, I promise I will make an appointment this week, but remember I am a nurse. It's probably just a bug going around." Slow steps towards the front door, she looked back and waved, "Let's go before we miss Youth Day. The kids will be so disappointed if you're not there."

The church had been seeking someone to lead the youth and who better than myself. Today was youth day which meant the kids took the lead in service. They were ushers guiding guests and visitors to their seats, their choir performed, they opened up in prayer, distributed communion, and sat in the pulpit with pastor. I could not be more proud as many of the fellow youth were from my center, some of their parents accompanying their children in support. Just in time for the choir selection, I watched as one of my youth from the center sang a beautiful solo, not a dry eye or member left in their seat.

Watching from a far, these kids had come so far in a matter of a few short months.

They sang beautifully, their prayers were powerful, and I could tell that many had an anointing of ministry on their lives. Despite being under the weather, I could tell that Mackenzie enjoyed service as much as I.

Today's service was entitled, Keep it Real. I could not deny, I got chills knowing there was a blessing to come from this powerful man of God. The sermon, lifting everyone out of their seats, spoke life to those who were and also those who were not keeping it real in life. One point in particular, hitting home for many, "Some folks, so quick to transform into something they're not just to put on this facade for temporary acceptance, let me tell you this," pastor said, "that acceptance was delivered and received under false pretense and will eventually be exposed."

Closing the sermon, pastor ended with this final point, "If we cannot be comfortable displaying our REAL selves, we will never receive God's blessing on our lives."

Service ending around two thirty, I gathered around my youth while my social butterfly Mackenzie, despite not feeling well, went and mingled with fellow church members. Beyond proud of these guys, I surprised them with the news that I was taking them out for lunch, pending their parent's approval.

Running this decision by Mackenzie, we wrapped up our separate conversations and headed towards the lobby. Mackenzie, a few steps ahead as I became the door holder awaiting the exit of Elder Jordan and a host of other members. My smile, greeting those who passed through the door, quickly transformed into fury, the sight in front of me anything, but pleasing.

Down the steps and near the parking lot, a small audience gathered around Mackenzie and an unknown male who was anything, but a man, the way he was shouting at my fiancé. "Lauren," he continued to call over and over while holding on to her arm. Relinquishing my role as the door holder, I had no choice, but to stand in between and protect my woman from yet a second man who mistook my fiancé for some woman who had obviously rubbed people the wrong way.

I didn't give a damn what any woman said or did, there was no excuse for any man to ever speak in the manner this punk was speaking. The fact that he was disrespecting my woman, who was my everything, you better believe he fucked with the wrong one. Leaping six steps down the stairwell, fearing not any injury I could sustain, in between the two of them I intervened. Chest to chest he and I stood, his only saving grace from knocking his ass out, the respect for both my lady and church family.

Taking a step back, I turned to console my fiancé who was visibly startled. Her hands trembling, facial features discolored, I asked even though I knew the answer, "Are you ok baby?"

Interrupting the conversation I was having with Mackenzie, this man, whom I had no clue the identity, grabbed my arm with such force that I tripped over my own two feet, facing his direction. Pounding his chest into mine, the argument he began with Mackenzie was now directed towards me, prompting Mackenzie to step aside.

Embedding his finger into my forehead, he began to shout. If we didn't have an audience before, we certainly had one now.

"Who the hell are you calling baby," he cursed.

The old Chris, before I became a saved soul, would have already handled this man street style. The Christian Chris; however, respectfully stood his ground, giving no further attention to this disturbed man's psychotic behaviors.

Introducing myself as he made it clear that he was not going anywhere anytime soon, I held my hand out hoping to redirect this hostility, "My name is Chris and you are?" Thinking if I gave him further insight, just maybe we could hold a man to man conversation and I could gain understanding as to his position.

Pointing to my right, I introduced, "This beautiful woman over here, the one you owe an apology for the way you spoke to her, she's my fiancé sir. Man to man, if there's something we need to discuss, I'm all for it, but you don't need to talk to her the way that you have." My position was firm, I'd stated my piece, and hopefully he understood where I was coming from.

He and I stood front and center of an entire congregation of onlookers. Jaws had fallen to the ground as this was not a daily scene one could expect to find in a church parking lot. There were a few phones out and I wouldn't doubt if we weren't on someone's snapchat, YouTube channel or live feed by now. Walking a fine line of physical contact, pushing me with his shoulder for the second and final time, this total stranger scrunched his face up and asked, "How the fuck can she be your fiancé when she is my wife?"

A gasp of air coming from the audience, I began to laugh hysterically at such a fictional tale this man concocted. Ironic, pastor had just preached a sermon about keeping it real and this man who stood before me, a mouth full of lies, couldn't be further from the truth.

Making sense of his nonsense, I shed some light on this deeply flawed individual, "If she was your wife sir, you would know her real name and it's not Lauren. Her name," pointing at my fiancé, "is Mackenzie."

My personal space invaded, he sought to further confuse me. "If she was your fiancé," pointing in the very direction I had, "you would know that her government name is Lauren Mackenzie Adams and that I," he spoke sarcastically, "am Marcus Adams, her husband. We have been married for the past three years." Giving this man no further attention, I walked over to my fiancé. Our bond was too strong for such a farfetched lie to be true. This man was on straight BS and I wasn't sticking around to entertain this hypocrisy.

Standing by my fiancé, I rubbed her elbow, ready to exit from this unnecessary scene of confusion. "Come on babe. Let's get out of here." This man had already made a fool of himself and I wasn't about to allow him to drag us along for the ride. Walking towards the car, assuming Mackenzie was by my side, I turned to find her frozen, her feet planted on the curb.

Overcome by fear, Mackenzie was unable to move. Stepping in as her knight in shining armor, I flew in like superman to save my angel. In the middle I positioned myself again, posing one question to Mackenzie. This question, once answered, would hopefully get this nutcase out of our lives for good.

Feeling silly allowing these words to flow from my mouth, I asked Mackenzie, hoping she wouldn't be too upset with me, "What he says isn't true, it is?" Had I been accused of doing anything to cause friction in my relationship by another woman and Mackenzie questioned me, I would probably be upset. For this reason, placing myself into her shoes, I would understand if she chose to give me the silent treatment for a period of time.

My only goal here was to display to the world that what this man was accusing was garbage. He had gathered a full audience and I wanted Mackenzie and I to be the ones to have the last laugh. I mean this had to be a joke. There was no way I had fallen in love with another man's wife. I mean we spent every moment together when she was in town. When could she have possibly had time to devote to another relationship? Between her business trips and time spent under my roof, it just didn't add up, did it?

Asking for a second time, "Baby, is there any truth to what this man is saying?" I hated the fact that our personal lives were on display for the world to view as their enjoyment. With much at stake here, all I could focus on was gaining the truth and not what others had to say.

"I would advise you to stop calling my wife baby," Marcus ordered, his warm breath felt on the back of my neck as he stood close. Intervening between the two of us, Marcus squeezed his body directly in front of Mackenzie where he reached for her left hand. Holding it high in the air, Marcus commented, "Now this ring looks nothing like the twenty-thousand-dollar ring I bought you. Where is it Lauren?"

You could see the smoke coming out of this man's nostrils. You could hear the pain in his voice. So convincing, I was in a position of playing tug of war with his accusations and her silence, but whose side would I lean?

When I met Mackenzie, she wore no wedding ring. When I met Mackenzie, she was not at all involved in any relationship as I made sure to ask before investing my heart. I didn't know what to think of her any longer, our entire relationship put into question.

As passionate as Marcus was, so too was I. Before I fought any further for this woman I wasn't sure I truly knew, I needed answers. I was not going to hold a conversation with a man I did not know. I didn't move him in to my place. I hadn't made love to him over and over again. There was no ring on his finger that I had given. We hadn't exchanged "I love you" towards one another. These milestones transpired between Mackenzie and I. She is the one who owed me some form of explanation as she had yet to deny a single accusation.

Mad as hell, finding it hard to keep my composure, I looked into the eyes of the woman I had fallen in love with who I thought loved me too. "Mackenzie, you have to say something." Pleading with her, "Please tell this man the truth."

"Yes Lauren, please tell this man the truth," Marcus mimicking my exact words.

Making no eye contact with either myself or Marcus, Mackenzie left me and a man claiming to be her husband, alone to sort out the pieces, possibly confirming the worst; she had been lying the entire time.

Never in my life had I been in any confrontation with another man over a woman I had feelings for. That behavior, in my mind, wasn't worth it and took accountability away from the person who equally promised to commit. On this day; however, it was safe to say that my feelings had the best of me. Reaching for Mackenzie's hand whom I could not bring myself to call Lauren, I was stopped in my tracks by Marcus. With full force, he slapped my hand away from Mackenzie's, a hand I had interlocked with for the last six months. A hand I kissed, caressed, consoled, and yearned to hold.

Like a thief in the night, Marcus yanked Mackenzie by the arm, pulling her far from me and in essence, pulling my heart as well. Trailing behind, Marcus stopped in his tracks, planting his feet firm into the cement. Mackenzie's hand bound to his, no opportunity to escape, he took two steps forward, his finger resurfacing in my face and commanded, "Stay the hell away from my wife. She is married and will not be seeing you again. This is the only time I will say this."

With a forced tug, he removed my world from in front of me, ordering Mackenzie, "Let's go now Lauren."

I had invested way too much into Mackenzie to see her carried off by another man without any closure or explanation on her behalf. I knew now that she was married as it was far too late to deny and although my mind started to accept this fact as reality, my heart did not understand.

My heart continued to crumble with each step she took through the parking lot. The pain, oh so deep knowing this may be the final image I have of her, almost transparent. Against better judgement, I ran halfway across the parking lot, joining the opposite side which her husband occupied. That side, containing her heart, my heart.

Feelings of regret would fester deep inside if I allowed her to walk out of my life forever, without telling her exactly how I felt. Hoping she would do the same, I disregarded her husband's presence and threats made, holding her hand firm inside of mine. Gazing into her eyes, filled with endless possibilities for the two of us, I began to cry, the pain of her leaving my life, a pain I could no longer hide.

Some may have seen me as a man in denial, but in actuality, I was a man of faith. I held on to the faith that this nightmare I was living was nothing more than a dream I was preparing to wake from. "Mackenzie. Tell me this is not real," the congregation following. "I love you and you said you loved me. We are supposed to be getting married baby."

Squeezing on to my hand, I held on to the ounce of hope that Mackenzie was genuine when she told me she loved me. I held on to the ounce of faith that instead of him, she would leave with me, where she belonged.

Paused for a moment in time, I was able to hold my baby's hand as she squeezed on to mine, our eyes making love, speaking the feelings our souls could not verbally release. In an abrupt manner, Mackenzie and I lost all body language shared, Marcus reappearing.

His toes aligned with mine, he reiterated words spoken which I paid no regard. He wasn't my father, my mother, or anyone else I owed a damn thing. He was a weak excuse for a husband who clearly wasn't taking care of home for his wife to search elsewhere.

I bucked up for I was no coward when it came to the one I loved.

Stepping back, he said, "I guess you didn't hear me just say back the fuck away from my wife bro."

What I recall next, his fist coming full force between my

eyes, my head bouncing off the pavement. My vision, temporarily distorted, I could hear out in the distance, a car door slam while making out the scent of rubber tires burning a hole in the ground as they sped off from the parking lot.

My lifeless body, resting on top of a bed of gravel, I found myself unable to move. This had all happened so fast that I remained in a state of shock. I hated to even think that my mother was possibly right about people hurting me down in New York, but look at me. None of this made sense.

Resting on the ground, my eyes closed shut, barely conscious, I could feel my arm being tugged at an upward angle. My head pounding, I lifted slowly up from the ground with the help of one of the deacons.

Batting my eyes open, the left socket hard to move, I could hear my youth group run up beside me. "Are you ok Mr. Harris," one of the girls frantically asked, wiping dirt off the back of my suit. Slightly dizzy, I turned to witness the entire congregation in awe; some attempting to hide their phones knowing they already posted an entire video for the world to see, speculate, and comment on my pain. Without even a word of goodbye, my heart had vanished into thin air. Familiar with her absence, having learned to cope, the exit this time one I knew was her final bow in which she would not be returning.

How could I tell my parents about this? I mean they loved her. My mother was so excited to finally have a daughter-in-law. How could she do this to me?

I was so angry and hurt at the same time, my efforts to hold back the tears, impossible. I didn't give a damn who was watching me. This pain I was experiencing, I wished on no one.

Thinking long and hard about our time together, certain actions I could now consider red flags that I allowed love to block. Our entire time together, especially after moving her stuff in, never, not once, did I see a hospital badge, nursing scrubs, the slightest utterance of her job that she supposedly loved so much and I certainly never saw her in action at an actual hospital.

How strange that I never met her family either. I mean, she did fill me in on the non-existent relationship she and her mother had, but what about her father? They were said to have shared such a bond with one another not easily broken; why was I never introduced?

I had glanced at her crying during service when the pastor talked about keeping it real and what I gathered as tears of joy stemmed from a moving service were actual burdens she had played on which had worked in her favor until now. Invested whole heartedly into this woman, never did I ask her to show me that I was just as important as I made her feel. I had given her ample opportunity to play this charade which probably would have continued up to our wedding day had her husband not found her. I'm not sure what tipped him off, but he must have been on to her for some time unless he was blinded by love as I was.

My entire being was Mackenzie. She had my heart in her hand and used it for her own good. I recall on our first date after church, asking her if she was seeing anyone else. She volunteered the fact that she was single while sitting across from me on my couch before we shared our first night of intimate passion. How could such a beautiful person outside be so deceiving on the inside? So much for meeting a good "Christian" woman in the house of the Lord as my mother requested. Removing myself from the paparazzi, better known as the church congregation, I escaped to my car as fast as I could in route of my house which was going to have to undergo many changes.

A silk robe instantly greeted me as I turned the key to unlock my front door. Laying perfectly along the couch, this the first item of hers making it even harder to clear my mind. Even the aroma in the air reminded me of Mackenzie or should I say,

Lauren. Dragging my feet along the hardwood flooring, I took baby steps into my bedroom where I threw myself face first onto the bed. My face buried in between the sheets, I must have pressed the mental rewind button in my brain because an instant replay of our passionate moments in this very bed, on top of these very sheets, fluttered in my mind. The entire bedroom was sprinkled with her memory which would make it that much harder to forget that she even existed.

I could see my boys now calling me soft, telling me to suck it up, or better yet, "Men aren't supposed to hurt," but the truth was; we hurt just like women, the only difference, there was some unwritten law that we were not supposed to display our pain. Damn the rules; men hurt and I was hurting bad man. I could not get my tears to stop for I was a man in love with someone whose entire existence was based on a lie. The worst part, as bad as I wanted to, I couldn't just turn off the love that I had for her. Even though she was someone else's wife which I didn't learn until after my heart was all the way in it, it didn't change the fact that I still loved and cared for her.

Slow jazz radiating throughout the surround sound of my speakers, each note piercing my soul, forcing tears to shower down as I laid across my bed crying. I knew that I was torturing myself listening to this genre of music, but in this moment, I had no care for anything or anyone. My head was low and I needed God to tell me why. Why would he allow a good man to get played? I'd done everything right. I found a woman in the church like my mother asked who she believed were the best ones. Before she and I went in any direction, I asked if she was seeing anyone. I respected her to the fullest, treating her like the queen I believed that she was. I rushed absolutely nothing with this woman placing no more on her than she was ready for and now everything was blown up in my face, myself the only one left to hurt. At least Marcus had her back.

I was all alone with no one to call my own.

CHAPTER FIFTEEN

Break Down

I opened my eyes to a familiar environment, a place that once had meaning and purpose, now a constant reminder of what was and will never be again. Pain inflicted by lies, betrayal, and deceit, I couldn't bring myself to climb out of bed and I most certainly could not answer any of my mother's phone calls, respectfully sending her straight to voicemail. The pain fresh, consuming all that I was, I had yet to expose the dark, hidden truth behind the fictitious relationship Mackenzie and I were involved. Nothing or no one could do anything to ease the pain I found nearly impossible to cope. I stood in close proximity of a flatline, the only resuscitation, a woman who had my heart in her hand, her heart belonging to someone else.

Hitting the snooze button for the third time, I made myself late for work and I just did not care. Staring up at the ceiling, I laid lifeless in the bed without as much as a blink of the eye. Reprogramming my mind not to look for routines I had made daily habits such as good morning texts, waking up in each other's arms, the scent of her cooking in the morning even if just a pot of coffee; these moments as small as they were, could not easily be erased from my thoughts. This entire morning unfamiliar, I found it much easier to throw the covers over my head, leave my blinds closed, and sit in the dark where I was alone, a relationship status I'd have to learn to adapt.

Thinking of my kids at the center, as much as I did not want to, I forced myself out of bed. Cold water dripping from the shower head, I sat in an upright position in the bathtub, the freezing temperature having no impact.

Pulling myself up from the tub, I walked over to the sink

where I stared at my reflection in the mirror. An appearance I did not recognize especially with an added bonus of a black eye. A black eye warranted as I allowed my undying love for a woman who's lies stood openly in my face and you know what, I wasn't mad at Marcus. Had he given me an opportunity to explain that I never entered into a relationship with Mackenzie knowing that she was married, just maybe things would have turned out differently. Even still, I sympathized with his pain. Standing here feeling sorry for myself, I could only imagine how he was feeling.

Consoling the view displayed in the mirror, I rubbed my eye in hopes that the blemish would disappear. Further irritating the wound, I had to think of another remedy to mask this very visible dark surface which the kids and possible office staff would reference. There was no way that I was going to escape the twenty-one-question game from Keenan. Knowing how his mind worked, he would think that I had gone to a club, fought someone for looking at me crazy, and curiously wonder if I got whooped as he liked to say or whooped somebody.

The reality of it all, there were no winners. All you had were two men, hurt beyond belief, both of which had a different way of displaying their pain.

My drive into work much slower this morning, struggling to even bring myself out into the public. My mind, barely focusing on the road ahead which appeared fogged, snapshots of the church parking lot episode so vivid so fresh.

A heart consumed by pain, held hostage, I just couldn't bring myself to revert back to the Chris I was prior to the public altercation that put my character and relationship into much question. I was far from a place of peace which I knew the world would have a field day with my open display of emotions that a reasonable person could not hide.

Whether it be the storyline of a drama filled movie, a talk show such as Maury, a male bashing R&B song, men were always and forever going to be portrayed as cheaters; women, the only victims in a relationship. Here I was, living proof that men could hurt just as bad as women with no one to share or run to during this pain. We men were supposed to take the blows as we probably deserved it. Well I, Christopher Harris did right by my woman. I loved her, cared for her, gave selflessly and here I was, a male on the receiving end of heart break.

Taking a deep breath pulling in to the parking lot of my job, I prepared my entrance, hoping to come straight through the door and into my office, no paparazzi, no questions asked. Crossing my fingers that no one was at the front desk this morning as I entered the building, I masked my eyes, the right one in particular with a pair of sunglasses that I would keep attached to my face until I made it through the double doors, down the hall, and into my office. A man on a mission, I opened the door and flew past any and all bystanders.

I was at the home stretch, my hand firmly cradling the office door handle. A slight breeze exiting the room as I cracked open the door, one foot inside the room. Lifting the other, I paused still, a chipper voice asking, "Chris. How was your weekend?"

Why Lord why? It was Justine in high spirits which I wasn't prepared. Regretting my arrival so shortly after all that had occurred which no one in this building was aware.

I contemplated taking the day off as I did not want to bring my personal inside of the work place. Seeing that even a simple question, inquiring about my weekend, triggered anger, I knew that I had to leave and fast.

Even in her absence, Mackenzie was affecting my entire life. My reputation destroyed at church, not sure if I would be welcomed to return. My living quarters, a haunting nightmare, each and every room a reminder of her in some fashion. Now she was affecting my attitude at my job. Sure I was responsible for my actions and behavior, but my wounds were open sores, the smallest things furthering my pain. I couldn't be myself anywhere as long as she was stuck in my head which I wished she wasn't.

Cautious with my word choice, as much as I did not want to speak for fear of snapping, I spoke brief. "Good morning," I said, keeping my eyes forward.

Laying her hand across my arm, Justine asked, "Are you ok Chris?"

Several follow up questions she asked, you would have thought with my one-word responses that she would get the hint that I was not in the mood for small talk, but apparently not as she continued to talk.

My eyes closed, hidden behind my sunglasses, I stood quiet, my shoulders rotating up and down as my frustration released in the form of heavy breaths taken. Justine was an amazing individual, but today, I needed her to back the hell away. Under my belt I held a strong work ethic, not once calling off, taking PTO, or conducting myself any less than that of professionalism. Today would be the first time ever, while employed in the company, that I had to take a personal day for the sake of us all.

Cutting in between Justine's words, "I do not mean to be rude Justine, but I am going to have to take a personal day off."

"But you just got here Chris. Besides," she pointed and stared, "Keenan has been anxiously awaiting your arrival. He made me promise to keep a secret, but he has something that he wants to show you."

Disregarding what I just said, Justine carried on in conversation, laughing aloud, "Keenan alerted everyone in the building the second you arrived to hold you hostage until he comes to free you."

I was held hostage alright, but not by Keenan, rather Justine's mouth. My hands trembling, I turned to face Justine for the first time since joining my side. No other alternative, I announced, "Justine, I just can't do this today."

Eyes burning, moisture seeping through my glasses, I began to cry in front of Justine, an act I was afraid of displaying. Angry, I thought, had she just taken the hint and shut up, just maybe I could have made it an entire day, left alone in my office to do busy work. Shaking my head, she just had to poke and pry.

Her mouth still running as I attempted to pass by, "Do you want to talk about it?" Breathing heavy, readjusting my glasses which turned into blinders, tears flowing into miniature beds of water along the rim, "I'd rather not. I'm going through some personal matters and I would prefer not to bring them into my work environment."

"We don't have to discuss it here. You say where and we'll go talk. Whatever you want to share Chris, I'll listen in support," she said, blocking my view of the exit door.

An uncontrollable amount of emotions, Justine prying herself into my life, now Keenan joining near, I made my exit, heading towards the front door as fast as I could allowing no further setbacks. "Mr. Harris, what's up? AH MAN, I got a A- on that math test," he shouted from the top of his lungs as I continued walking.

Life entirely too much to handle, I had to temporarily ignore Keenan as much as I did not want to. Excited I was to learn of Kennan's accomplishments, first-hand knowledge to how hard he worked, I was terribly saddened also and the two emotions combined, just did not create an atmosphere of positivity. This Chris, lonely, confused, dazed, unwelcoming was not me at all and I couldn't apologize enough for those who had been exposed, all the more reason I had to disappear for a while. Awaiting some form of acknowledgment, I turned my back on Keenan, hoping and praying that I had not lost his trust or respect.

"Keenan, Mr. Harris will be right back ok," Justine comforted.

Justine was right, I was coming back, just not today.

Trying hard to lose her, Justine followed as I made my escape out of the building and towards my car. My keys falling to the ground as I stood near the driver door, it was Justine who lent a helping hand, leaning forward to retrieve, but not return my keys. Over and over again, she offered a shoulder to cry on and as much as I tried to fight it, I was starting to feel that I could use one.

Bringing myself to the realization that I could not fight this battle alone, I lowered my guard, Justine's offer of moral support, a start to my healing process. Arms outstretched, it was Justine's entire persona that made the acceptance of her support one of ease. Although the tears resurfaced, I felt protected in Justine's arms. In this moment she wasn't my boss, but a friend who had my back to the fullest which I appreciated even though I was unable to express my gratitude at the moment.

Holding me close, Justine whispered in my ear, "Men hurt too Chris and its ok to let it out." Revealing not one detail about yesterday, as if Justine were aware that Mackenzie was the root of my problems, she said, "I do not know who she is or what she's done, but if she has put you through this much pain; you don't need her. Someone out there is ready to love you as you love them and they'll make you appreciate this day for this is a day to let go and let God work." I must have had heartbreak written all over my face, Justine's words hitting home. Using my sunglasses to block the untold story, I slowly lowered them off my face, completely comfortable sharing everything with Justine.

Granted the time that I needed to get myself together so that I could prove myself as a counselor and staff member, I looked Justine in the eye, no longer afraid or nervous to display my mark and promised to return better than ever especially for my man Keenan.

CHAPTER SIXTEEN

Responsibility

I had gone a month without Lauren and yes, I was finally in a place where her government name could roll off my tongue without feeling the urge to break down and cry. Still, a long road ahead, I was getting better one day at a time.

Four weeks, two days, thirteen hours and conveniently enough, Lauren appeared in the inbox of my text messages. An action that once brought me much excitement now a feeling of disgust. There was absolutely nothing that we had to talk about, no common link that would bind us together. Forced to glance at the portion of the message that appeared on the screen of my phone, Lauren wanted to inform me that she had recently changed her phone number in efforts to create a fresh start as if I cared one bit. I too was working diligently to look past all that attempted to bring me down and this fresh start of mine as she sought to create for herself, had no room for a woman of trickery.

Responding not a single text message, Lauren appeared in the inbox folder of my email account as if she hadn't gotten the hint that I was through with her. Scrolling through the content, in search of two words, I'M SORRY, I sent all ten messages which lacked importance, into the trash folder where I permanently erased them. My eyes baffled, Lauren had the nerve to input a signature at the bottom of her messages with a name, Mackenzie. This woman was a trip.

It was clear that she only had herself in mind, thinking not of the pain that she had caused and left behind. Her husband would probably flip the hell out, if they were still married which did not concern me, had he been made aware that she was reaching out to me. This, all the more reason I ignored any involvement.

I left myself so vulnerable to her that I overlooked the possibility that she was not being truthful in our relationship and the price I paid, I got played. Without a doubt, this was a lesson learned, one I'd never forget.

What I will say which I will not beat myself up for, I showed this woman how she was supposed to be treated. She did not want, need, or have to ask for anything because I personified all that a man should be. I observed my father's display of care and affection towards my mother my entire life and his actions, I carried into my relationship.

When I first laid my eyes on Lauren, I saw something special which I desired to have. So special that I stopped at nothing to pursue her. Looking in the mirror today and after all that I've been through, I realize that I put my all into the wrong woman and I'm cool with that reality. In relationships you have to take chances; you win some and lose which is all a part of putting yourself out there.

While I was nursing myself back to the Chris everyone knew and loved, I held on to Marcus in my mind. Sure enough I was hurt over Lauren's actions, but Marcus was the one who was married to her. Lauren took a vow before God and I could only image how life was working out for him since the heartbreak I'm sure he too, had endured. We were two men in love with a different woman who wore the same outside appearance. She was Mackenzie to me, but Lauren to him. When she was on her so-called business trips away from me, Marcus held her, touched her, soothed her pain, and when away from her husband, I repeated his actions. I wished that he and I could have sat down rather than resorting to violence and public humiliation, but as they say, heat of passion distorts the mind causing uncontrollable reckless behavior and on that day, we were both deeply flawed which I have much regret.

Delivering a public apology to all church members, the first step in the right direction as I began to press forward in my life. A single man now, I was able to devote more time to the church and ministries in need of assistance. Not only was I the youth leader, but I became a church mentor for young men who had been released from prison unsure of how to redefine themselves. I could not relate in a sense of being a former inmate, but I had grown up with numerous friends who had been in and out and in again and it was their stories that I was able to share. As far as redefining themselves, well that allowed me to use my degree and together, we were going to see some positive changes. Ironically, they had come to me for help not knowing, they were actually helping me as well.

I had packed all of Lauren's belongings that I allowed her to store in my home. This gesture, a sign of commitment to only her. Each box containing a memory I wanted to leave in the past, I placed out of sight and in a vacant room, buried pain.

It felt good to breathe again, to smile again, to live again. Time on my hands, I met and joined a group of guys, all belonging to the ministry, Single Men of Christ. This group proved to be uplifting, inspiring, each of us with similarities we could learn and grow from as a brotherhood. My brothers in Christ, they too were a healing force. Asking God for guidance, I remained focused, what was most important; myself. Had I remained in a state of depression a moment longer, simply allowing life to pass me by, I would have given someone power that they were not worthy, nor did they deserve.

My job, a nonprofit, forced me to do a lot of networking which I enjoyed. My charm back in affect, I had persuaded a few agencies to listen to a proposal in hopes to receive additional funding for maintenance around the center. The meeting, held in the center's gymnasium, the perfect spot that even the blind could see the poor conditions forced to occupy. I added not only visual appeal, but a slight personal touch as I explained how I wanted to impact the lives of these children as they had very little hope to hold on to.

The center was the only meeting place many of our youth could receive transportation to and from school. This was also the only facility that would feed them both breakfast and dinner, should they have to stay late. Little to no funding, we were desperately seeking outside help to keep the facility up and running. Surrounded by facial expressions of all sorts in the room, I was not sure if the crowd truly valued or even understood the importance of maintaining a danger free environment for these children. My prayer was that someone out there could in fact relate to some of the struggles these children faced, tugging on their emotional senses, leaving a burning desire to give.

My tactics, implemented strong, in a matter of an hour and a half, the grant money was ours, not a dry eye in the room. Justine, beyond ecstatic, invited the staff including myself, out for drinks to celebrate a worthy moment for our center.

Hesitant at first, I decided to accept the offer and celebrate with my coworkers after such an accomplishment. The center had been saved, no one aware, but the staff, that it was up for possible closure if not brought up to code by the state. A sigh of relief, we now had the funding which also meant a weight lifted from each of our shoulders to stress no further.

After work, just before meeting my coworkers at a local pub in the city, I retreated to my patio, a routine that remained the same. This time which I often looked up to the clouds, my opportunity to talk to God, I used to lay each and every burden down.

I could complain about being alone or having my heart broken, but what good would that do? My heart may have been broken, but I refused to allow the actions of another to break me. God had brought me out of the storm and by his grace, I was still standing with my head held high. Looking back at all that God had shielded me from, an instant reflection of Mike surfaced through my mind. The sun beginning to set, the moon slightly visible, this setting an exact replica of that night he was murdered.

The images clear in my mind, it made no sense that I wasn't lying next to him, six feet under in the cemetery.

He called me around six that night and asked if I wanted to hoop. The two of us, like Shaq and Kobe, I was always his right-hand man on the court. We had to have played for about four hours before we fell to the ground, tired as hell. *Dappin* it up with the normal crew that ran with us, Mike and I drug our feet step by step towards the car that was so close, yet so far away. As I climbed in the front passenger seat, barely able to lift a muscle, I noticed Mike detour in the opposite direction, walking away from the car in route of two unfamiliar faces I'd never seen before.

The conversation couldn't have lasted more than a couple of minutes which is why I didn't think anything of it at first. His energy replenished as if he hadn't just run seven games with me, Mike jumped in the driver seat and asked, "Ay man, take this run with me and then we'll go get some eats."

Thinking to myself, this fool must have been crazy to think I was going to carry my funky ass anywhere without a shower. Taking a whiff of my shirt, drenched in sweat, "Bro, you can't be serious. At least let me run home and take a shower first." Starting the car, he turned to me and begged, "Come on bro. It will only take a minute. I swear, pretty boys always worry about every little detail," Mike continued, no sign of running me home.

It was no secret the lifestyle Mike carried, which is why I never asked for any details. I just laid low and drove with his cry baby self, "Shut up whining fool. Let's go and there better not be any females there." The entire structure of Mike's face now serious as he began looking back and forth at his phone, I began to wonder if this run had anything to do with the dudes he was talking to at the court.

Slapping the side of his right arm, an act I knew would piss him off, I asked, "Those dudes you were talking to, I've never seen them hoop with us before. You know them or something?"

Rubbing his head with the most concerned look, one I'd never seen before, he responded, "Naw, but they wanted to know if I had any Kush. You know what they say, scared money don't make money." Now I didn't know much about the game, but I knew enough to know not to sell to people you didn't even know. I mean what if they were the Feds or stick up kids. I had to knock some sense into Mike before we drove any further.

My tone stern, "Bro. You don't even know them."

Mike had come so far and here we were a few short months from going off to college, I couldn't stand to see my boy go down the wrong path over a poor choice. "You know we are about to head off to college. Leave that shit alone before you find yourself in some mess you won't be able to get out of."

Rubbing my head in a childish manner, Mike began to laugh, "I didn't know you cared so much." He was playing, but I was dead serious. Pushing his hand far away from my head, I shouted, "I mean it Mike."

Contemplating for a moment or two, I could see his brain cells connecting the dots, hopefully close enough that he would turn around and focus more on his future and not his past which was always getting him into trouble.

"I feel you Chris," staring at the rearview mirror. "This is the last time and then I'm out. I swear."

Looking over at each other, I actually believed that I made a difference and hopefully knocked some sense into Mike. We had too many future plans together, none of which could be carried out if he found himself behind bars.

In close distance of the meeting spot, I'll never forget the change of plans which ultimately saved my life while my father fought for his. I remember my mother calling me, frantic. She told me that my father had been rushed to the hospital as he collapsed on the kitchen floor, complaining of chest pains. The worry, displayed on my face, Mike busted a U-turn and took me straight to the hospital, putting his business on hold. Mike, about as close to my father as I, offered to stay, assisting where needed. This type of call, one you'd never want to receive, had me nervous, unable to process anything anyone had to say which is why I told Mike he could go on without me, no idea I'd soon be going on without him.

Most concerned about my father's well-being, I forgot to tell Mike to be careful. Promising this, the last sell he'd ever make, I knew that he would be alright and that we'd be off to college soon, together.

Within two hours, the doctors had entered the waiting room and with much relief, informed that my father was going to pull through. Remaining in the hospital for observation, mom and I returned home for some much-needed sleep.

I could hear the house phone ring all the way from the driveway of our home, the calls nonstop. It had to be after two in the morning and even still, this person would not stop calling. Unlocking the front door, my mother jogged to the nearest landline in the living room while I closed and secured the door behind. Assuming it was either dad, wondering where we were as he was sound asleep when we departed or a family member checking in after learning of dad's near-death experience, I left the call to mom and headed up the stairs to my room.

My right foot barely grazing the third step of the stairwell, I could hear my mother's somber tone, question, "Oh Lord. How am I going to tell Chris?"

My feet planted on the hardwood, my mother

approached, silent cries she could not keep to herself. Wrapping her arms around me, she began to rub my back, whispering into my ear, "I'm so sorry honey." All I could think, my emotions not yet unleashed, not my dad. Her head in my chest, she shook her head from side to side and with a muffled tone, "We're going to get through this baby."

Staying strong for my mother, I held her close, whispering back, "I've got you mom." Guiding me down the steps, into the living room where she asked me to have a seat, "Sit down baby."

Revealing her pain stricken face, she squeezed my hand, her lips quivering. Choking on her words, she lowered her head, "I'm so very sorry honey."

Although visibly hurt, this hurt a different appearance than that of losing a spouse, my mindset redirected. Asking a question, I believed I knew the answer, I took a deep breath in, exhaling it slow, "Is it Mike?"

Releasing the tight hold she once held, she rested her hand on my shoulder, her eyes positioned in front of mine, and confirmed my worst fear, "He's dead baby. Someone shot him."

Anything said or done after that moment, a complete blur. All I remember was kissing my mother on the forehead and walking upstairs to my bedroom where I quietly shut my door and cried myself to sleep. I didn't care how tough anyone expected me to be, Mike wasn't just my best friend, but a brother I never had and I wasn't hiding my tears for anyone. I spent so much time after his death blaming myself for not being there by his side as I'd been many times before, this internal battle, one I could not express to my parents. This exposure, one that would uncover Mike's activities, I felt unnecessary.

Since his passing, I've made sure to visit his grave every year on the exact day of his death, allowing nothing to stand in the way. I wondered what he would have thought of the whole

Lauren fiasco if he were here. Knowing him, he would have told me never to fall in love in the first place.

This coming from a person who had no plans of ever committing to one woman for more than a week's time.

Man, we had some good times, great laughs, and memories to last a lifetime.

Retreating back inside the house, feeling myself slipping into an emotional episode, I forced myself to get dressed in hopes of having a nice time celebrating with those I was certain would lift my spirits. A day like today, I needed good vibes my way. My keys misplaced, I went on a brief search before heading towards the front door. My hand firmly surrounding the door knob and on the opposite side, a soft knock rattled.

Assuming they had the wrong address as I was not expecting company, I refrained from answering the door, allowing the stranger to realize they were at the wrong home. Knocks continued, I pulled the door back slow, removing the barrier which blocked myself and the unknown visitor from a meeting of the eyes.

"Hello Chris. May I come in," the uninvited visitor requested.

The visual, one I did not expect nor want to see.

I had not replied to one email, responded not a single text message, or accept a phone call and still, this woman had the audacity to step into my life as if I would welcome her with open arms. There was nothing left here for Lauren except a couple of boxes which I would gladly send with her as she turned and walked in the other direction, far away from me.

Enunciating loud and clear a response to her request to enter inside my home, prepared to slam my door closed, immediately following the word rolling from my tongue, "NO." A desire to apply force to my door, hitting Lauren smack in the face, I instead, guided the door gently with my hand. Slight resistance as my door would not latch, it was Lauren, from the opposite side, attempting to pry the door open. Expressing some form of urgency, "I really do need to speak with you." I honestly did not care what she had to say, but so she would have no reason to return, I gave her a minute of my time, literally, to speak. No need to yell, argue, or point the finger, I remained calm, "Mackenzie, Lauren or whatever you go by, I have nothing to say to you and I couldn't imagine what it is you need to say to me after all this time."

I could further this conversation adding the fact that she was a liar, had yet to apologize, and could have potentially ruined my life, but that would make her think that I cared or held on to some sort of emotional attachment which was untrue. I was doing just fine and the sooner she left, the faster I could go back to my new-found state of serenity.

Distance maintained, she said, "I'm asking for ten minutes of your time and then I promise I'll leave." I didn't want to give her one second and here she was, asking for ten minutes. What the hell kind of conversation was going to take ten minutes to state? Little did she know, this so-called conversation was going to be a monologue, not a dialogue.

Did she fix her lips to make a promise? Now I was mad, anger I didn't think I had, resurfaced which I gladly directed towards this woman. "Don't you ever fix your lips to promise me anything. I don't trust one word that comes out of your mouth." I had worked way too hard to get this woman out of my mind and heart and I was not about to back track now. She could save her lies for the next man.

"Chris please don't make this hard for me. What I have to say is very important," she expressed, her hand outstretched, which I moved away.

Did this psycho just say don't make this hard? Oh I wouldn't dream of making life hard for Mackenzie, I mean

Lauren.

Helping herself to the cushion of my couch, a couch that I did not invite her to sit on nor did I want her to get comfortable. Time ticking away, what could be so important that she could not express via text, email, or voicemail which was nothing more than small talk that I declined? Keeping the front door company, preparing to watch as Lauren exited, myself trailing behind, but in the opposite direction, I motioned with my hand for her to get to the point.

Dragging her words and feet, Lauren began to walk around the couch, touring with her eyes, my condo. "The place looks just as I remember it."

Irritated, "Lauren I have someone I need to be with. Are you going to tell me why you're in my house?"

In front of me she now stood, her fingers slowly moving down my chest, "You look very nice. Who is the lucky lady?"

Did this trick just touch me and have the nerve to ask if I were going on a date as if that was any of her business? She was the married one, not me. In fact, why did I have a married woman in my house anyway? Opening the front door further, "I do not owe you any explanation. I really need you to go so that I can celebrate with my friends. Let's cut the small talk."

Her eyes bright, "What are you celebrating?"

"LAUREN," I shouted.

Grasping the fact that what once moved and soothed me no longer had an impact, her words began to pick up in speed. "Ok. Do you remember when I got real sick and you told me that I should probably go and see a doctor," she asked. A confused look I displayed, a participant now of the memory lane game, I played along, but not for long. "How could I forget? I was right by your side, wasn't I?"

Staring off into the distance, "Yes you were."

Not sure where she was going with this conversation, I asked, "Why are you bringing this up?" Don't misunderstand, I was not cold at heart, but this woman had taken me through the ringer and still without apology. Here she was expecting to hold a conversation as if we were buddy-buddy again.

"You kept telling me to go to a doctor which at first I didn't until recently." Feeling like I was going to be here all night, I rested my back on the wall near the front door and with a roll of the eye, I replied, "Ok." Her words hard to hear, she said, "Chris, I'm pregnant." The words, in one ear and out of the other like a shooting star, I asked for her to roll the tape back, "Come again?"

Her hands held together in praying form as if she were some sort of innocent church girl, nodding her head, she repeated, "I'm pregnant. Three months to be exact." Idle I stood, not exactly sure how to process such untimely, not yet proven information. Lauren was not the one for me, in fact, she wasn't my woman at all placing serious doubt and suspicion in my head.

Willing and prepared to take care of my responsibility as a man, I wasn't quite ready to sign on the dotted line underneath the title, daddy, without further proof. Lauren had spoken enough, now it was time that I start asking some questions of my own.

"Considering the bullshit you put me through, how in the world do I know that the baby you are carrying is mine," I rightfully asked. My mother raised me to take care of my responsibility. My father raised me to be a man, neither one raising me to be a fool. She may have played me once, but as the saying goes, "fool me once, shame on you, fool me twice, shame on me."

A valid question I do believe for anyone who had ever

been in my situation, a question she clearly took offense, she spoke with much hostility, "Are you accusing me of something Chris?" Removing my back from the wall, I stood tall, delivering my response not as a deadbeat, but a man more than willing to step up once the truth was confirmed.

Pointing the finger directly into her scope, "The one thing you are not going to do in my own house is play the victim. I have every right to ask that question and I want an honest answer. How the hell do you know that the baby is mine considering the fact that you are," my hands up in the air, sarcastic expression painted on my face, "oh I don't know, MARRIED?"

Pulling a piece of paper from her purse, which I never personally saw the contents, looking down she answered, "Once the pregnancy was confirmed, the doctor collected blood samples and determined that the time of conception happened to be spot on with the time my husband was away. He was actually in Houston for an annual Firefighters Recognition Banquet, leaving you, Chris."

Her words alone were not valid in my eye. In fact, I demanded to see this mysterious document which did in fact point an exact timeframe of conception. Indeed, she was pregnant which begged me to question if in fact I had implanted my first child inside the womb of a married woman. This was some Jerry Springer, Maury type of mess that I did not want to be in.

Both hands on my knees as I leaned forward, my thoughts racing, I could only imagine what words Marcus had for me. Breathing out of my nostrils, I questioned, "What does Marcus have to say about this? Surely he can't be pleased." Startled at the sound of her husband's name, her feet completely lifted from the ground, Lauren asked, "How do you know my husband's name?"

Were we not all huddled in a kumbaya triangle in front

of the church? Was she not standing directly in front of the confrontation brought on by her lies prompting her husband's actions? If my recollection of memory was not enough to jog hers, maybe the permanent scar under my eyeball would bring it all back, "Oh, he introduced himself just before punching me in my face thanks to you."

An unsettling sigh released, I'm sure it was only a matter of time before Marcus and I met again, the circumstances this time, worse than the first encounter.

"Considering we are now separated, he is not saying much of anything. He knows I'm pregnant," she offered.

With her track record, I needed a much more detailed response. Guiding the conversation, I asked, "But does he know that he is not the father? Surely that didn't go over very well. " Eye contact lost, she softly stated, looking away, "Yes. He kicked me out because of it." It bothered me that she was incapable of making eye contact as if she were still hiding information from me. She spent more time looking at me when she was lying than now, claiming to be truthful.

Unable to carry the weight now placed on my shoulders, I became weak at the knees, unable to stand any longer. Lowering myself into a chair near the couch, I asked, "So where have you been staying since he kicked you out?"

I did not care where Lauren was staying or even if she had a pillow to rest her head at night, what I did care if in fact the results were true, was the well-being of my unborn child which unfortunately, Lauren happened to be carrying.

"Sometimes I stay with my dad, hotels often, and when I'm at work, I rest in the lounge," Lauren informed.

Her eyes, off to the distance, I could see her chest slowly rise up and down, "Tonight will be the first ever, that I have to sleep in my car. Not only did he kick me out, but he cut off all access to our joint account, containing both his money and mine." Closing my eyes, holding in the longest breath ever, I released from my mouth, words I knew would eventually backfire, I just wasn't sure when.

"This is -," contemplating whether or not I was going to proceed in conversation, "This is definitely not how I envisioned bringing a child into the world, but we have to play the cards we were dealt. With that being said," I stood in front of her, making a vow I planned to stick to, "you got me. I don't want my child to ever feel that his or her father wasn't a significant part of their life. Each and every doctor's appointment, I'm there. If I can help it, you will have a stress-free pregnancy."

My personal feelings no longer relevant, I had to start thinking like a father. I had in fact slept with Lauren unprotected, ignoring the "what could" happen. We equally played a role in the conception of our child and had to come together as one in order to ensure a safe and healthy pregnancy. Blowing air within my cheeks, swooshing my mouth around, I thought long and hard as I prepared to pitch an idea, an idea that even I could not believe I was about to suggest.

With my back turned, facing the nearest escape route, I could in fact avoid the offer I was preparing to place on the table. Thinking of my unborn child, I saw no other choice, but, "If you would like, you can stay in one of the spare bedrooms."

So that my kindness wasn't mistaken for weakness, I made one fact very clear, eliminating any and all confusion, "You staying here is for the sake of our child, that is all. I want absolutely nothing to do with you on a romantic level. Please respect what I'm saying."

Allowing Lauren to remain under the same roof was for the purpose of our child only. Any fantasy she had nestled in her mind about pursuing any form of romance or rekindling a past I had finally gotten past, she need not express and/or attempt to act upon because I wasn't going there.

Showing her first sign of misunderstanding, Lauren leaned in, wrapping her entire body around me which I corrected with a quickness. Redirecting her arms to her side, I stepped back and reminded, "Lauren, please respect my wishes. What we had is gone. It will never be again. From this moment on, our priority is the child that you are carrying. " Shifting her face to a look of discomfort, Lauren rejected the invitation to stay in my home. "I think I'm just going to go Chris. I do not want to impose. I just wanted to tell you face to face about the pregnancy. Now that you know, I think it's best if I go." That somber tone, those puppy dog eyes, and her mastery of the art of acting may have worked on others, but I was not moved.

"So what, you plan on sleeping in your car," I reminded.

"You don't want me so I guess I have no choice," her head hanging over her shoulders.

In a high volume, stern voice, "You are damn right I don't want you. I want the safety of my child which should be your thought as well. I would advise you to start thinking like a responsible adult seeing that you are now carrying another life." Frustrated, I turned to my watch realizing I'd been going back and forth with Lauren for over an hour now. Revisiting my front door, a door I should have walked through sixty minutes ago, I cut my words short. Concluding the conversation, I asked Lauren a very simple question which required a yes or no only. "Are you going to stay or not?"

Looking down at my watch again, "I have somewhere that I have to be and if you are going to leave, I need to lock up behind you." Agreeing to stay as if she had any other logical option, I removed from my key ring, one of the two copies I had to the front door, placing it both carefully and fearfully into

Lauren's palm. Hesitant to accept, she asked, "Are you sure you do not mind me staying? I really can leave." I absolutely did not want her to stay, but this was not about me, but our child. Whatever I had to do for my son or daughter, I was prepared to do.

Exiting the front door, I couldn't quite figure out how to process this overload of information I was forced to accept. Just when I felt like myself again, the pain a distant memory, here she was again with news binding us together for the next eighteen years. Was I really about to be a father? I could only image what my parents would say once I gathered the courage to tell them. They had no idea that the woman they grew to love was indeed an imposture. They sure as heck didn't know that she was already married, a shock to me as well. To their knowledge, we were planning our wedding together. So much I had to tell them; their response, one of my worst fears. Contemplating whether or not to stay home for the evening, adjusting to my new roommate, I realized that I could not let all of my coworkers down. This was a celebratory night for all of us, one I was not going to let Lauren ruin.

By the time I stepped in the room, it was clear that everyone was feeling their liquor. We had gathered at a small little hang out spot called the Avenue which was known for their drinks and live band performances. It felt good to get out and relax and for a short while, blocking out the fact that the one person who turned my life upside down, would be in my home once I returned.

Making myself comfortable, I threw back a couple of shots with some of my coworkers while we sat and enjoyed each other's company.

As much fun as I was having, there just weren't enough drinks to go around to entirely block out the unknown direction my life was preparing to take. Desperately seeking the advice of someone wiser than myself, I thought of my father, but I just didn't know where to begin. Thanking everyone for the time spent, I excused myself from the fun everyone else was having that I could not quite join in.

As late as it was, I walked in the house quietly as if I were sneaking into my parent's home after curfew. Now this was my house which I could do as I pleased; however, I was mindful of my new move in roommate. I stepped into my room, in search of a pair of shorts and t-shirt to sleep in and with the glare of the hallway light, I could see a faint shadow of Lauren, sound asleep in my bed. The hallway light not enough to aid me near my closet, for a brief moment, I had to turn on the ceiling light. Fighting the urge upon exiting my walk-in closet, I could not help, but stare at Lauren, outstretched across my bed. She had made herself comfortable in the very spot she had many times before, this time more beautiful than ever now that she was carrying my child.

How did I go from hating this woman so much to mild feelings for her all over again? Confused I was, my mind and heart not in sync with one another. Did I still love her? Torn between jumping in the bed alongside of my former fiancé, I gathered a t-shirt, shorts, blanket, and pillow as fast as I could and headed full speed out of the room.

In close contact of the couch, I could hear fast paced footsteps towards my bedroom. These steps as though they were on a mission, forcing me to turn around and check things out. Lauren no longer in the bed, a trail of light leading to the nearby bathroom. An unpleasant, gurgling sound followed by a splash of water and from a distance I could see Lauren struggle to lift from the floor as she flushed the toilet. Rising from a forward position near the sink, a reflection of Lauren's eyes displayed on the medicine cabinet, holding on to her stomach, she stood and asked, "Did I wake you Chris? I'm sorry."

Taking a few steps further into the bathroom, I reached for a roll of paper towels under the sink where I began to clean remnants of throw up surrounding the toilet. Turning away, my stomach too weak to look down, I said, trying to keep a straight face, "It's fine. Are you ok?"

Her face pale, eyes flushed, "I'll be ok. The first trimester has been pretty tough, but I'll make it." First trimester what? How many trimesters were there? I was going to need a book of translation to get me through all of these pregnancy terms.

Offering my shoulder, Lauren too weak to keep her head up, I assisted her into the bed where she seemed to be at peace.

Falling fast asleep, I swung Lauren's legs onto the bed as they dangled on the side of the mattress. Reaching on the opposite side of the bed, I grabbed my comforter and made certain she was nestled tight. Back to the living room couch I returned, popping in on Lauren ever so often.

Soon, I too, was off to sleep.

THE NEXT MORNING

A familiar scent in the air had stimulated my sense of smell, but where was this aroma coming from?

The smell comforting, sure to heal any wound bringing one to a state of serenity at just one bite.

Lured onto my feet, I rose from the couch which I slept uncomfortably all night and with my eyes, witnessed Lauren standing over the kitchen stove.

Forced into the kitchen, hunger pains piercing my abdomen, I hid my curiosity, reaching past Lauren for a glass of water when in fact I wanted to put my hands in each dish she presented beautifully on the counter. Into the refrigerator, I searched, pretending there was no scent or display visible which I could indulge.

My heart jumped, surprised to find Lauren hidden

behind the refrigerator as I closed it shut, a container of yogurt in my hand. The yogurt, no match for the plate of food which sat directly under my nostrils. In her hand, Lauren held onto a sample filled fork which she brought closer and closer towards the center of my lips. Visibly better than last night, Lauren demonstrated a burst of energy as she directed, "Try this. I made a quiche, sausage, pancakes, and fresh orange juice." As much as I wanted to lick the fork clean, I politely declined the offer, resorting to my eight-ounce container of yogurt. Leaving her alone in the kitchen, I excused myself where I retreated to my bedroom.

In a disappointed voice, I could hear Lauren speak, "The food is in the kitchen if you get hungry," the sound of the fork hitting the bottom of the sink. Pouting upon consumption of each spoonful of yogurt, I had to decline Lauren's cooking. She and I were still figuring things out as far as parenting and I was still trying to wrap my mind around the fact that she was back into my life after fighting so hard to get her out. Excepting her food would further confuse our situation and possibly bring hope into Lauren's eyes where there was none, another reason I was skeptic about our public outing this afternoon.

Unable to endure the discomfort in my back, I offered to take Lauren shopping for a mattress and bedframe in effort to regain ownership of my room and allow her access to one of the other vacants. Make no mistake, had she returned to my doorstep without child, you could bet every penny, we would not be in the process of shopping. The fact that she was carrying my son or daughter meant that I had to make certain, their mother was well taken care of.

Approached by an older woman in the furniture store, Lauren and I both received compliments on our appearance as a good-looking couple, the elder carrying an angelic expression on her face. "You two remind me of myself and my late husband. You are truly a beautiful couple."

As much as I wanted to correct the confused woman, the

fact that she compared me to her late husband, I had to keep my comments to myself. If Lauren and I weren't already distanced from one another while in the store, you better believe that comment furthered my steps clear across the store. Allowing a service rep to somewhat stand in my position, I pointed towards Lauren, asking the gentleman to assist her with the selection of a mattress. Asking my price range before introducing himself to Lauren, I made it clear that I did not care especially if I was going to gain from this shopping experience, peace of mind.

"The total today will be $1,039.87," the cashier said.

Looking down into my wallet, slowly retrieving my debit card from its compartment, I was in complete dismay at the fact that I was spending this amount of money on a woman who wasn't even my woman. Perturbed, I followed the prompt while swiping my debit card, asking a very important question, "When should I expect the bed to arrive?" Skimming through the computer, she responded with much hesitation which had me unconvinced, "Ummm it looks like we have a truck available for drop off the day after tomorrow. Will morning or afternoon work best for you sir?"

Today would have been a better response, but I guess two days was much better than weeks of waiting and aching on the couch.

A sigh of relief, I stood near the door ready to exit only Lauren was nowhere to be found. Organized by departments, I began searching throughout the aisles of the store for Lauren. Pacing up and down each row, I watched as Lauren stood motionless, her hand resting on one specific crib in the nursery department. Observing the selection of cribs myself, familiarizing myself with what would soon be a near future purchase, I found myself ready to faint into one of the adjacent rocking chairs at some of these prices.

Clearing my throat, practically choking at these prices

as if we were at a car dealership. Catching my balance, I rested my back on a crib that had its price tag turned around. For laughs and giggles, I readjusted the sales tag which read, marked down to $1400, originally $1699. Grabbing my chest, I swiftly walked over to Lauren and asked, "Are you ready to go?"

Her words battling the actions of her eye sight, she answered with much uncertainty, "I guess so." Leading the way, Lauren walked a few steps in front, allowing me time to secretly snap an image of the crib that had all of her attention.

Not at all impressed with the price; I was however, willing to sacrifice for my child. The car ride too quiet, radio filled with commercials, I looked over at the passenger side seat to find Lauren's eyes in direct view of my very own. Leading in conversation, I asked, "Why are you so quiet?"

Cradling her stomach with one hand, the other stroking it up and down, she responded with much sadness, "It just hit me that I am going to be someone's mother soon and I'm not exactly sure how. My mother was never there for me and I don't know the first thing about caring for another life." This moment, the perfect time to attack Lauren who had infringed much pain on both her husband and myself. The nerve she had to blame her upbringing for why she could not be a good mother to our child, I had no sympathy for.

Putting a stop to the "woe is me" pity party, I revealed a hidden truth to Lauren, one I had only shared with Mike. This exposure, I sought to use as an intervention, a ray of hope that she could in fact be a good mother to our child despite circumstances.

My eyes focused on the road, I cleared my throat, and out of my mouth, I released a family secret. "What many do not know about me is that the man I call my dad is not my biological father. My real father left my mother when she was eight months pregnant, leaving her without physical, emotional, or financial support and I'm still standing. The man I call my dad, came into my life when I was three years old. Not once have I allowed the absence of my biological father to hinder all that I could be as a man. I've made no excuses for the direction of my life based on my lack thereof and you don't have to either." Time and time again as a psychologist, I sat down and listened to lack of accountability and excuses made for the direction lives traveled, including Lauren and I could not help, but to get upset. "It blows my mind listening to people blame each downfall on what they lacked growing up. We are each accountable for our own actions and cannot allow our upbringing to be used as a crutch for where we are," I stressed.

My eyes taken off the road for a split second, I looked over at Lauren, hoping to get through to her. "Your mother wasn't a vital part of your life, ok. Are you going to blame every step you take on her absence? I did not have my biological father in my life, but I didn't allow what he missed out on to interfere with the enjoyment of life."

Hitting my steering wheel, feelings exposed, "You have the opportunity to be a great mother Lauren, but first, you have to start by being honest with those you love and/or care for." Eyes back on the road, in essence looking out to the future, I spoke one piece of advice to the mother of my child as we returned home. "The choice is yours to make the most of the life you live. You can either let it consume you and bring you down or strengthen and aid in endless possibilities."

CHAPTER SEVENTEEN

Under Different Circumstances

Thanks to much prayer, I had fully adjusted to living under the same roof with the woman I vowed to forget. No longer holding on to any grudges, I was making it through, one day at a time making sure that the mother of my child was happy and well taken care of. Preparing our son's arrival, Lauren and I were in a place where the entrance into co-parenting would be a breeze.

A man of my word, I was there for each and every doctor's visit. I held Lauren's hand through all exams, cradled her at night when the pain was unbearable, and lent my support, however needed, so that she would never feel alone or without. Utilizing the third bedroom, Lauren and I worked as a team to transition a blank canvas into a beautiful animal themed nursery for our son. Coming to a joint agreement that we would not have a baby shower, I made certain that all baby necessities were on hand. Lauren's stomach growing, the visual on the ultrasound monitor, the tiny clothing in the closet, this all surreal until the crib arrived. Putting in quite a bit of overtime, I surprised Lauren with the crib she could not take her eyes away from. The two of us in a much better place, I was honored to see her happy because if she was happy that meant that my son was happy.

Even though I had not yet held my son in the palm of my hands, the feelings I formed for him were indescribable. I loved this little boy beyond measure and he couldn't get here fast enough. This sense of happiness also came with a state of fear. Fatherhood was new to me and I wanted to be the best at it, but with the unknown direction of life which I already gathered a glimpse, could I be all that my son needed me to be as his father?

As far as my personal life was concerned, dating was simply out of the question. Although Lauren and I were not a couple and had not shared one intimate moment since she moved in, explaining the entire situation to any woman I found interest, was a story not even I would believe. Come on now, for me to tell a woman that the mother of my child was living with me simply because I wanted to be involved in each stage of pregnancy, there's no way on earth they wouldn't think Lauren and I had an attachment beyond a child and that there was no sexual activity. Lauren and my child were my extracurricular activity, anything else would have to take a backseat. Fearing she would lose the baby traveling and working long hours on her feet, both Lauren and I agreed she no longer work through the duration of her pregnancy.

Taking much stress off where I could, I made it a routine to come home from work and make dinner, giving Lauren the opportunity to prop her feet up and relax.

With each step Lauren took around the house, I felt tempted to lay my hand on her stomach and rest my head near any movement just to be near my son. Fearing these moments would be misconstrued as acts of romance, I often found myself turning in the opposite direction, only staring at my son from a far distance.

This distance I was forced to feel was nothing compared to the distance I kept my mother and father who still had no idea that they would soon be grandma and grandpa. Missing out on so much already, I could only image the pain my mother would feel not being able to host a baby shower or share in learning the sex of her grandson. Babies were her world whether she knew them or not. She was always giving back to the community as we didn't grow up with much and I just couldn't stand to break her heart.

These last few months in which I used to heal my heart and accept this new-found life, I hoped and prayed my parents would understand the distance. I wanted so bad to rise above this defeat on my own without my parents holding my hand. You could not have told me that I would set out to New York, fall head over heels for a woman that was married, and also father a child with her. These details, once exposed, may very well place a gap in the bond my mother and I shared and possibly my father as well.

My son's arrival less than five weeks away, I was finally prepared to face the music. Taking a few days off from work, I set out on a three-day road trip to sit face to face and come clean with my parents. No matter the end result, I could no longer hide this information. If I wanted to be treated like a man, the reason I took a leap of faith out to New York, I would have to stand up as a man. My parents not yet aware of the news they would soon find out, there was one person I could confide in. This person, the least judgmental, one who knew all that was going on in my life; Justine.

I felt it only right, after breaking down in the parking lot, to express to someone, the heavy heart that broke me inside and out. In preparation to walk the line of fire, I asked Justine out for lunch as I did not want my personal business circulating around the office. Her smile radiant as we sat across from one another in the booth, it was this display that helped me get through all that had consumed me since my arrival to New York.

Using the toe of her high heal shoe, Justine grazed my shin, and asked, "So what's going on with you and Mackenzie? I'm sorry, I mean Lauren." Justine, as close of a friend as Mike was, I let her shade slide. Always full of energy and personality, it was hard to believe she was battling anything internally, her exterior surface always in good spirits.

Responding with a crack of a smile, "Oh you got jokes."

Changing her tone, more serious this time, "I'm for real. How are you holding up?" I couldn't recall the last time someone asked me how I was doing as it pertained to the events that took place with Lauren and I. Whether it be the church congregation, who had a front row seat to the unfolding of the truth or even Justine until know, I rewound the tape briefly, and with confidence, responded, "Honestly, I'm good. She and I are doing what we have to for the sake of our son, but other than that, we keep our distance. I don't see her the way I did when we were together if you can believe that."

Smiling inside, I repeated my response in my mind. A refreshed feeling, almost as though I had rededicated my life to Christ, I confirmed my verbal response with a head nod and repeated, "I'm really good Justine." Leaning forward on the table, squinting her eyes together, Justine pointed a fork in my direction and asked, "Then what's the problem Christopher?" Was it written across my face? Embarrassed to come clean, I rubbed my hands down my face, stopping at my lips. My response muffled, both hands blocking my mouth, "I still haven't told my parents that she's pregnant."

"Tell me you are joking right," she responded. I wished that I was joking, but I wasn't and I needed her advice on how to come clean. My head down in shame, I responded, "I just haven't found the right words." The more I thought about all that I was hiding from my parents the more it ate my up inside. My parents and I were extremely close and secrets, we just didn't keep.

Reaching for my hands, Justine held them close as they rested on the table and spoke blunt. "You're going to have to help me understand why you would hide this news from them Chris. I mean, they are your parents and they deserve to know how you are doing and what is going on in your life. Please don't think that I'm judging you, but aside from being your boss, I'm also your friend. It's one thing not to tell them that you two ended the engagement, keeping this facade that you're still together, but to keep from them that you will be a father, why?"

This Justine who sat across from me today, I hadn't been formally introduced, but I needed her honesty. I also needed to explain, this my first practice go before I went before my parents. Subconsciously rubbing Justine's palm, "When I moved down here I promised that I would handle any obstacles on my own and not reach out to my mom and dad to take care of me."

"The fact that I had sex, unprotected at that, I had already gone against the Christian values I was brought up. From this act, one I knew the consequence, a child, how well do you think that would go over? The worst part of it all, hey mom and dad, not only did Lauren who you know to be Mackenzie and I have sex numerous times, we're having a baby, and oh, did I mention, we can't get married as planned because she's already someone else's wife. Yeah, that would be a smooth conversation."

Justine's eyes could cut my drama filled life with a knife. Valuing our talks, I took heed to her opinion, one I knew was festering the second I placed a period at the end of my explanation. "As much as you say that you feel your time here has been of many embarrassing moments, these moments were not caused by you, but another. Mackenzie was not Mackenzie, but Lauren. You fell in love and did right by a woman who did not appreciate or value your love to speak the truth from the beginning. Your entire relationship rested on a foundation of lies."

From a distance, I could see Justine become emotional, her eyes taking on a foggy appearance. Pulling her hands off of the table, crossing them on to her chest, she spoke with much passion. "Chris, she even had your parents fooled and for that, I'm sure they will welcome you with open arms. Tell them what's going on not just because they're your parents, but think of all the stress it will eliminate, the weight you will no longer be forced to carry. " Just the person I needed to prepare me mentally to face my parents, Justine had removed each and every jitter within. No matter what they had to say, I knew that my parents loved me and that together, we were going to overcome this patch in life.

Prepared to hit the road, I had one final question Justine could help me answer. "Do you think I should bring Lauren on this trip," I asked.

Shifting her lips around as though she were filtering and choosing her words wisely, Justine spoke, "You know that I support you and I would never state anything that would hurt you, but I am going to be completely honest on this one; it's time for Lauren to step the hell up. It seems that everyone has allowed her to stand idle in the background, owning up to nothing she has done or the pain she has caused. That day I witnessed your heart, broken outside of your chest, I wanted to kill that bitch for hurting you. For her to not even apologize after all you have done and continue to do for her, the least she can do is stand before your parents and explain to them, what she has done rather than you having to face them alone."

Putting on hold the worries in my head, I focused on my Beef Manhattan which arrived hot, the scent, delightful. With a nice plate of food and good friend to keep me company, I saw no point in dwelling on the unknown. I knew that God was going to see me through which is why I put my worry to rest. Justine hardly touching her plate, mine halfway gone, it seemed that she and I switched roles for a change. My worries put to rest, her facial expression showed that something was eating away at her.

Removing the napkin from her lap, Justine sat it on the table as an indicator that she was finished with her food. Clearing her throat, she looked at me, her eyes filled with mystery, stating, "I want to share something with you Chris. You don't have to respond, just listen."

Background noise taking place of the silence that stood between Justine and the confession she wanted to make, I waited. Focusing in on the sapphire necklace that rose up and down on her chest as she took in heavy breaths, still no word in sight.

Her eyes closed, a soft breeze exiting the tiny opening of her lips, Justine revealed what she could no longer conceal.

"I think I'm in love with you Chris. Our bond has developed into much more than I ever imagined. In every way that you have been to Lauren, I've yearned to find the same characteristics in a man of my own," she exhaled again.

Her palm on my wrist, Justine reminded, "Please don't feel pressured to respond. I just had to get this off my chest."

My jaw face first on the table, my mind racing a mile a minute, I was unsure of what to say. Justine was beautiful both inside and out. We shared so much time together and never, not once did I get the vibe that she was interested in me beyond a friendship.

"Wow," all I could think to say.

Yanking her hand back, "Being that I am your supervisor, this information, I never planned to share. You may be concerned about future dating with your current situation, but I assure you, any good woman will look past all that you believe to be a deal breaker. You're a good man Chris and there is a good woman out there just waiting on you." I became further tongue tied with each word Justine spoke so confidently. She was fearless and here I was, fearful. My life was in such disarray and I honestly wasn't looking for a new relationship or in a rush to have my heart broken again. At this moment in my life, it would be unfair to bring Justine into a world of confusion. Sure Lauren and I were cordial at the moment, but we had yet to discuss life after the arrival of our son.

Praying my response would not damage the friendship we shared, I carried myself and my plate next to Justine. Laying my head on her shoulder, a friendly gesture, I allowed my heart to do the talking.

"You are beautiful and that is undeniable, but I'm in no shape to start a brand-new relationship," I confessed.

Placing an innocent kiss to the back of her hand which I held, "I would love to see where you and I could go if we entered into a relationship, but right now with the arrival of my son, Lauren still under my roof, I just can't give you all of me no matter how much I would like."

Comfortably resting her head on top of mine which hadn't yet left her shoulder, she responded, "I completely understand and appreciate your honesty. If you and I never end up together, I want you to be happy Chris." I cannot recall whether or not our heads ever lifted from the moment we shared or if we even finished our food. All I took from what was supposed to be a meeting seeking advice, Justine wanted to be with me and deep inside, I wanted to be with her. If we were meant to be together, fate would bring us back together.

CHAPTER EIGHTEEN

I Am A Man

The gear shift in drive, my foot pressed heavy on the gas, I was quickly approaching the driveway of my parents' home, the trip shorter in distance than ever before. Against the advisement of Justine, I took this drive solo, leaving Lauren behind.

Under false pretense, my parents had been made to believe that life with Mackenzie was nothing less than perfect. As I explained to mom each time she called and inquired an update on our nuptials, the busy schedule Mackenzie and I had, my mother took it upon herself to take over the planning portion of our wedding which I didn't have the heart to tell her to stop.

Less than ten feet in distance, it was time to strap on my boots and go forward with what I set out to do.

"Hey Mom and Dad," I said.

Seeing my mother and father in the flesh was a mixture of fresh and toxic air. I was overcome with joy just seeing their smiling faces. My mother's hands reaching out to me, I eased in close, longing for this moment where I could return into her arms. "Well hello stranger. You must be extremely occupied with Ms. Mackenzie that you can't even give your mother a call anymore," she spoke in a sarcastic tone.

My facial expression blocked by her warm interaction, I thought to myself; if only she knew. Standing over the stove in the kitchen, my mother asked, "Are you hungry son?"

In a hurry to confess to my parents all that had been

kept inside, I refrained from stopping to eat while on the road. I was very much hungry which gave me an idea. As much as I longed for my mother's cooking, I took it upon myself to invite my parents out to lunch. I knew that in a more public setting there would be less cause for a dramatized response which I knew my mother was capable of executing. My charm, which had never failed me before, I used to lure my mother out of the house. Reaching for her hand which held a spatula, I rubbed her wrist with my thumb, glanced at her with puppy dog eyes, and suggested, "You're always cooking ma'. Why don't I take you and dad out, my treat."

Not a second thought, my father ran straight for the front door, so fast you could see smoke igniting from under his heels. The car ride quiet, give or take one or two intercessions, mom telling me to slow down, dad ordering mom to pipe down. Moments like this really had me missing home. Accompanying me to my final meal, I offered my parents the choice of where we ate. My father's mouthwatering for BBQ, we entered into one of my favorite mom and pop rib shacks up the road where many childhood memories were held. Holding the door open for both of them, my hand began to tremble as I reached for the handle which drew moms attention.

"Chris. Your hand. Are you feeling well son," a concerned mom asked. Guided to our seats by the hostess, mom trailing close behind as she wasn't convinced that I was indeed ok which I confessed.

Menu's awaiting our arrival as they sat on the table, I watched as mom and dad focused all of their attention on the contents inside, giving me reason to believe that if I spoke fast enough, just maybe the words would fly over their heads and we could continue having a beautiful lunch. Clearing my throat, "There is something I need to talk to you guys about." Recalling the saying, "out of sight, out of mind," the moment I disclosed that I had something I wished to share, my mother's menu flew across the table out of sight, never to think of again. Leaning over the table, eyes popping out of each socket, she asked, "What is it Christopher? Are you sick baby?"

Christopher was code for who the hell messed with my baby. My thumb and index finger, coddling my lips as I went on an internal manhunt, in search of the right words. The spotlight already on me, I was starting to think that I should have brought Lauren after all. Releasing the air from my body like a fully inflated balloon, the time had come. There was no turning back and so I let go and let God lead the direction of my words.

Unable to block the emotion which also hindered the deciphering of my verbiage, "When I left for New York, I left with the intent to better myself as a man. I left wanting to make the two of you prouder than the day you watched me graduate college. I found a dream job, a home to call my own, I was going to church, and I even found, what I thought was a great woman."

My mother, interrupting any further conversation, covered my hand with the palm of hers, asking very direct, "Why isn't Mackenzie a great woman? You two still are engaged to be married, correct?" The pain no longer until my mother asked the status of our marriage. Emotions overflowing, I begged my mother to pause any further interruption and allow me to finish stating what was on my mind.

"Please let me finish mother," I requested.

Dad, upright in his seat, leaned in close as well, asking my mother to chill. "Michelle, be quiet and let him speak. Go on son."

"After our second date, a moment did not go by without me thinking of her. Wanting to demonstrate the depths of my feelings, I asked her to move in with me which she agreed." My mother's jaw on the ground, her lips watering to speak, I held my hand up and put to rest her inquiry which I could see on top of her forehead. "Before you ask mom, yes, we were having unprotected sex."

Lowering my head on the table, burying my face into my arms, I began to sob as I revealed, "She hurt me so bad."

A hand resting on top of my head, positioned face first into the table, "Was she seeing someone else? Did she hurt my baby?" My father, disgruntled with my mother's constant butting in, had yet to utter one word until now. "Michelle, let this boy talk. Can't you see he's trying to get it out?"

Covered in tears, I lifted my head from the table, ready to meet my fate. There was no turning back, no exit door to escape, no one to phone home. Staring at mom who began biting her nails, now over at dad who sat with his arms crossed, I counted to three and said, "She is seven months pregnant with your grandchild." Both faces frozen still, processing the words I just spoke, my mother asked low, reaching in for my hand as a means to console my pain, "Did she just tell you this?" Making the story worse, I had to admit to withholding this information.

"No. I've known for about four months now," I sighed.

"For the past four months, we've talked with you son and every time I've asked how you are doing. Not one time did you ever say that something was wrong especially something like this. Why would you keep this from us," she asked, her eyes squinted together. Throwing my back onto the cushion of the booth, my hands in the air, "Mom, she is married."

There, I said it. It was out in the open.

A cloud of smoke pouring out of her nostrils, "Out of all of this, what hurts most as your mother is the fact that you believed you could not come to either of us. We are your parents and we love and support you no matter what mistakes you make in life. Mothers always know when something is not right. The distance you kept, the short phone calls lasting no more than ten minutes, Chris I knew something wasn't right. As much as I wanted to pry, I also wanted to give you your space to reach out as you saw fit. A part of becoming a man is being true to yourself as well as others. Even a man cannot walk through life on his own. At some point, you need someone and you have us, right Leroy?"

Nudging my father, who displayed a look I'd never seen and honestly feared. Drying my face with a nearby napkin I grabbed from the dispenser, "What does your husband have to say about this mom?"

Holding his hands together which rest on the table, he began to bite down on his bottom lip as he asked, "I'm just curious, what does her husband have to say about all of this?" Looking out into the distance, I began to replay the day in the parking lot where my life changed drastically. "Let's just say there was more physical contact than there was verbal communication."

"What does that mean," dad shouted.

Pointing underneath my eye socket, a blemish, noticeable to anyone who approached, "He punched me in my face, right here under my eye." I could tell that my mother was locked and loaded, ready for the person who struck me in the face. Even at the age of twenty-three, my mother was always ready for war when it came to her one and only son. I'll never forget the day she dropped me off in middle school and saw someone steal my lunchbox. Before I could even defend myself, she had gotten out of the car, her keys still in the ignition, just to grab my lunch back.

Away from the table my father's eyes wandered; what was once a party of three dialogue was now a conversation between my mother and myself, my father no longer partaking. Slapping my dad in the back of his neck, my mother asked, "Leroy, as much mouth as you have, say something to your son. Don't just ignore him."

A frown painted on his face, "I'm not sure what to say Michelle. Are you ready to be a father Chris?" Not a fan of my father's tone, I kept my composure and respectfully responded, "The baby is coming whether I'm ready or not. I just want to do the right thing."

"She is married as you said. How do you know this is your child," my father asked with his eyebrows raised. Unaware of why I was receiving so much hostility from the man who taught me never to run from my responsibilities, I continued listening to his opinion, a fuse away from responding in an unpleasant tone.

"The date of conception matches the time that she and I were together," I clarified. "Does she have any papers to back her story," he imposed. Pulling from the hat, one of the many lessons I learned growing up, I reminded my father, "She told me and had the papers to back it up."

Rubbing his head, my father spoke, "Son, she lied to you for months. Who is to say that she is not lying now about the father of this child? Anyone can make conception forms online. She could have easily written her conception date on that paper. I do not want you raising a child that's not yours." Coming from the very many who raised me, fully aware that I was not his biological son, "You raised me," I reminded. Pounding his fist onto the table, an entire restaurant of onlookers, "Do not make this about me. There is a big difference there. I raised you with no lies hidden. I did not come into the picture until after you were born and I've loved you ever since. Your story and mine are nowhere near the same," he shouted.

Raising my voice in return, a temper within I was unaware that I even had, I responded to his finger pointing. "Dad, I would rather be man enough to actively participate in the pregnancy than to distance myself and find out that he is mine and I was not there."

"You just didn't want to use your brain did you," my father asked. "Leroy," my mother interjected. "What did you say Leroy," I snapped. This was the first time ever, that I called my father by his first name. I was so angry that I wasn't thinking straight and at this moment, emotions high, he better be glad that's all I called him. Brushing her hand against my arm in an aggressive manner, my mother shouted, "Chris, do not call your father by his first name. Show some respect."

Looking around the restaurant, all eyes on our booth, my mother reminded, "You two settle down. We are in public." Both hands balled into fists on the table, my father spoke, "No Michelle. Christopher is a man now. Let him tell Leroy how he feels since he's such a tough guy." Standing away from the table, pounding my fist into my left hand, "I am a god damn man and I know that I am doing what is right whether you like it or not."

Shouting, I continued, "I would never turn my back on my child. Give me some credit." Applauding sarcastically, "Sure Chris, I'll give you credit. You knocked up a married woman and now you believe the child that she is carrying is yours. Hey everyone, a round of applause for my son Chris on his major success." Did he really have the entire restaurant cheering for me as if I won an award? These were not the words of my father, but a man whom I did not know. Taking all that I could, I felt it best that I leave before anything else was said that I may regret.

Leaning in, I gave my mother a goodbye kiss as she remained seated in the booth. "Mom, I'm going to leave now," ignoring my father who sat beside her.

A woman of peace, my mother pushed past my father like she played defense on the football field, in effort to speak with me alone. Holding my hand in her right, my father's in her left, she spoke, allowing her eyes to circulate from my side to his, "you two need to calm down. You have both said some things you shouldn't have and right now emotions are high.

Chris, please sit down honey. We hardly get to see you. We are a family and we are going to get through this together."

"Isn't that right Leroy," she tugged on my father's fingers.

"Speak for yourself Michelle," he snarled.

This response, one without reason, signaled me to exit the restaurant deeming this trip, a disaster.

Regaining ownership of my hand which my mother held hostage, I leaned in for a drive by kiss and exited the building, giving not one fuck about my father. "Goodbye Mom. I will call you when I get home," I promised.

In a hurry to leave, I could hear my mother speaking behind me, but who she was directing her comment, I did not know nor care at the moment.

LEROY & MICHELLE

"Leroy. How could you talk to our son that way? It took so much for him to tell us what was going on. You saw how broken he was and instead of being his father, you talked to him like he was dirt on the street. You couldn't even put yourself in his shoes for even a second. He may never come to us for help again. Shame on you. You couldn't even tell him you loved him."

"Michelle, Chris has been my son since he was three. Of course I love him. I have done all that I can do to see that he grows into the man I want him to be."

"Stop yourself right there. Chris will never be the man that you want him to be because he is not you. He will be the man that God intends for him to be."

CHAPTER NINETEEN

The Bigger Person

I could hear my father and I going back and forth like children in a heated conversation, stating painful dialogue we both regret. My temper flared, I wasn't the least bit excited to return home to Lauren who happened to be the root of the problem. There she was as I unlocked the door from the outside, sitting on the couch, feeding her face. As rude as it seemed, I walked past her like I was back to occupying the house to myself. Fearing that I would take all of my frustration out on her, I declined any and all conversation for the time being.

Straight to the kitchen I went, searching for something strong enough to take the edge away. Lauren, tiptoeing behind, was saved by the beer bottle held between my lips which blocked all unfiltered words I so desperately wanted to release. My back turned, she was also saved by the biggest rollercoaster eye roll my pupils gave as she attempted to start a conversation. "How was your trip Chris," she hopped around like the energizer bunny. Did she not get the hint that I did not want to talk nor see her? Throwing my beer back as fast as I could, I just couldn't relax.

Pestering me about my trip, I focused my eyes on her while resting my elbows on the counter. In the most unpleasant tone, I spoke, "Lauren, I do not want to talk about it so back off." Mortified that yet again, I was in a hostile situation on account of her actions, all bets were off and my words, no longer silent. Standing straight, "You know, I should have brought you along and just maybe, that would have taken much of the heat away from me. That is how it went."

Pointing my finger, "My father and I may never speak to each other again because of you." Rubbing her stomach as she did any time her demons were exposed, she asked, "Do you want me to go Chris?"

Screaming to the top of the ceiling, annoyed as hell, my mind filled with mixed emotions, I just couldn't take it. "Stop with the sympathy act. You are not the victim. As a matter of fact, I am still waiting on an apology from you for putting me through all of this shit. I have never argued with my father before so I gladly give you every bit of thanks for that." Holding her hands midway in the air, a form of surrender, she said just before parting, "I will just go in my room and leave you alone."

What she did, where she went, I did not care. Waving my hand in her direction, I turned my back, my eyes no longer forced to bear witness to Lauren's existence. "You do that Mackenzie. Oh I'm sorry, I meant Lauren," I corrected as she walked away.

The nerve of her to play someone's victim as if she earned that badge of honor. Thanks to her, I could now add a second, hostile confrontation onto my resume. For this woman, I felt the least bit of sympathy. All I ever wanted was to make my family proud of the man that I had worked so hard to become. I did not want to worry them with my mistakes here in New York which is one of the reasons that I waited so long to speak up. In my heart, I was doing the right thing by moving Lauren in for the time being and assisting any way that I could with the pregnancy. If she said that the baby was mine, I believed her. Who would lie about the father of their child? I mean, Lauren failed me in many ways, but she was not dumb enough to lie about something so serious.

Unable to decipher whether or not the three beers I had consumed or my conscience was making me think, after a long hour resting on the couch, I began to think about the way I spoke to Lauren. I did have every right to be mad at her, but I had no right to yell or disrespect the mother of my child. For that, I needed to go and apologize immediately.

Standing in front of the bedroom door which allowed no entry as it remained closed, I gave three faint knocks, asking, "May I come in?"

"Do what you want. This isn't my door nor my room," Lauren responded from the other side of the door.

She was correct, the door I stood before was not hers, but as a guest in my home, I wasn't just going to barge in without permission.

Walking in slow, preparing my words, I sat on the edge of the bed. While she lay on her side, her eyes staring at the wall, I stepped up as the bigger person, "Look, I'm sorry if I upset you. I am not used to arguing with my family. I'm under a great deal of stress right now, but I'm man enough to say that the way I spoke to you was wrong and for that, I'm sorry Lauren."

Her eyes now watering, her body moving side to side, I hoped she wasn't about to start crying. Grabbing on to her stomach, she uncomfortably shouted, "OUCH."

"Ouch what," I panicked. Panting, she spoke, "I'm not feeling very well." Slouched over in the bed, I rushed to her aid unsure of what to do other than be there.

"What's going on Lauren," I asked with much concern.

Breathing in heavy, her words muffled, "I'm not sure, but my stomach is cramping really bad."

Guiding her onto the pillows near the headboard, I ran to grab my phone. Wanting to call my mother, our distance was entirely too far for her to lend any assistance which is why I contacted our OB instead.

Shouting with much pain as she lay uncomfortably

across the bed, "HURRY CHRIS." Instructed to time the contractions by the doctor on call, it was determined that what Lauren was experiencing where Braxton Hicks, also known as false labor pains. The contractions too far apart to head for the hospital, I stayed up to monitor both Lauren and the baby. Upon request, I slept in the same bed as Lauren, my arm wrapped around my son. For the first time ever, in the midst of offering my security and support, I felt tiny little thumps kicking away at my wrist.

Whispering in her ear, I asked, "Lauren, what's that?"

Turning slightly, our eyes reunited, "that's your son kicking."

Overcome by much excitement, I couldn't help, but close any gap that stood between Lauren and I. Anything to further connect with my son, I was prepared to do even if that meant I had to hold Lauren all night long. The movements nonstop, I began to worry if I caused the false labor pains Lauren was forced to endure. I could never live with myself if anything happened to my son. Even though my little man could not hear me inside of his mother's womb, I connected with him, rubbing the exterior shell that kept him safe throughout the entire night. Hoping he could feel my presence, I wanted him to know that I wasn't going anywhere, ever.

WELL RESTED

The sun shining bright, unveiling a brand-new day and our son remained nestled inside the womb. Thank God we were out of the danger zone.

Lauren doing much better, I stood before her and vowed to never allow myself to go into such a state of darkness where I lashed out.

Avoiding time off until the baby had actually arrived, I

made the decision to go into work, but not before reminding Lauren to contact me even if the pain was minor. I wasn't taking any chances as Lauren's due date was just around the corner.

Justine brought up to speed on the horrendous dinner I had with my parents as well as my burst of anger, leading to what could have very well been a home birth, she remained my friend, judging not. As I should, I took ownership for my actions, pointing the finger at no one, but myself.

Displaying similar character traits of my mother, Justine always stepped in to be the peacemaker. In her mind, where there was a will, there was a way. Pitching the idea that I should take Lauren out to dinner as a friendly gesture, I couldn't help, but inquire if Justine was sick in the head. She knew everything about our relationship, stood witness to me cry on her shoulder like a baby, and out of all remedies, dinner was the best she could come up with. Making no promises, I kept my ears open to this farce of an idea.

"Before you go turning your nose up, hear me out Chris. You do not have to like nor love this woman, but as the mother of your child, you take strides to improve your relationship to establish a healthy environment for your child together," Justine reasoned.

Her words never anything short of selfless, I couldn't help, but think of how amazing Justine truly was. Even though she knew we could not be together, Justine still had my back. She held my hand when I could not see and supported me whether right or wrong.

Hesitant at first, I agreed to Justine's idea and asked Lauren out to dinner as friends.

What could dinner hurt? It was just dinner, right?

CHAPTER TWENTY

No More Lies

Returning home from work and boy was I exhausted. As much as I wanted to postpone our dinner outing, Lauren was already getting dressed and I didn't have the heart to cancel. If I noticed anything about the mother of my child as she furthered in her pregnancy, it was how slow she moved. Tonight, I was more than willing to accept her slow rate in pace for this would allow me time to close my eyes on the couch while she finished getting ready.

Rest and relaxation not on my side, I remained wide awake, fighting both the knots in the couch having a field day with my back and the vibration of my phone going off on the coffee table. My eyes wide open, a quick nap no longer an option, I reached for my phone to find that I had four missed calls and two urgent voicemails from my mother. This night just kept getting better and better. As God is my witness, I loved my mother dearly, but I was in no mood to hear her attempt to rationalize what my father said. The urgent messages, I'm sure were nothing more than a tactic to get me to call right back. This evening, a farewell parting to our nights of sleep, I wanted to focus on rebuilding with Lauren. The past, no longer a focus for we were walking into our future as mother and father.

Taking the advice of my dear friend Justine, I extended this dinner invitation which Lauren happily accepted.

Finally dressed, I escorted Lauren to the front door, asking as she waddled slow, "Are you sure you're ready?"

Although she did not find the humor, it was hilarious

watching her walk around the house like a little duckling. In a place where the two of us could laugh together again, I made reference to the mismatch shoes Lauren had on her feet. "The last time I checked, a blue sandal and red sandal did not match unless you're trying to be patriotic," I laughed.

Offering my assistance, I searched the bedroom for a mate to one of the two shoes she wore. Deciding to go with the red, I assisted Lauren as she attempted to remove and replace the blue shoe, her stomach interfering with her ability to lean forward.

Our car rides no longer silent and awkward, instead they were very much entertaining. Divided by more than the center console while occupying both the driver and front passenger seat, Lauren and I were divided by baby names as well. Lauren selecting names such as Diesel, Dakota, and Bronxx, while I appreciated one's uniqueness, I couldn't help, but fear that such names would cause our son to be passed over by employers. In my mind I thought of strong names such as Jackson, Jameson, and Xavier. Until we could both agree on a fitting name for our son, he would remain Baby Boy Harris.

While adjusting my rear-view mirror as we were in route to dinner, I couldn't help, but notice a dark colored charger riding my bumper. Fearing if I pressed on the brakes, he or she would run right into the back of us, I picked up speed.

"Do you see this crazy car behind us Lauren," I asked.

Unable to readjust her body in the front seat, Lauren instead, rolled the window down and glanced out of the passenger door mirror. Staring brief, Lauren began to laugh as she rolled the window back up, "Maybe you are driving too slow old man."

The safety of Lauren and my child, all that rested in my mind, I was happily prepared to allow this nut of a driver to pass us by. His or her speed, far beyond the limit, was certain to cause an accident if they did not slow down.

Hunger kicked in as if it ever left, Lauren asked, "So Mr. Harris, where are we going for dinner?"

My response, interrupted by the seventh call from my mother, I placed my phone into the cup holder where I planned to keep it the remainder of the evening. Returning back to the hungry mother's question, "I thought we would go back to Nixon Square. I remember how much you loved their menu."

Her mind, obviously redirected from my gesture of a friend, forced an act of intimacy out of her. What started as a cradle of her hand around my wrist, transitioned into a sneak attack towards my inner thigh. Hand entirely too close to my scrotum, causing me to swerve one good time, Lauren batted her eyes, recalling, "How could I forget Nixon Square? That is where we shared our first meal, first slow dance, and had our first date."

She was clearly misinformed about this night. Removing her hand, I shed light on my intentions for the evening so that there was no further confusion. Carrying her wrist by the tips of my fingers, I repositioned her hand back over to her side of the car.

Speaking firm, I cleared up any misconceptions, "Lauren, let's be clear. I did not bring you out this evening for the purpose of going on a date. As the mother of my child, I appreciate you and simply want to thank you for all that you have endured while carrying our son."

"Do you ever think about us? The passionate nights we made love, holding each other close as we slept in one another's arms, the dreams we shared," she drifted. Lifting my butt up out of my seat, an escape route from her out of control hands, I again, explained my position.

"In the beginning, I couldn't get the thought of you out

of my head. As much as I hurt, I still yearned for you. From your soft touch, the warmth of your body, the scent of your favorite perfume lingering around my room and then reality came crashing down. I knew that if we ever came in contact again after that day in the parking lot, the trust was gone and the feelings that once had me floating on thin air, were much like a balloon released into the sky, never to be seen again," I spoke honestly.

Focused less on the silence that had returned between us, I was more concerned with the same nut that continued to trail behind me. Making the decision to switch lanes, I blew out a sigh of relief as the driver was no longer in sight. He or she was either in a hurry, under the influence, or just crazy in the head. Whatever the case, I was just glad they were gone.

No longer focused on what was behind me, my eyes were set on the brightly lit Nixon Square, displayed ahead. Street parking completely occupied, we were redirected behind the building, where thankfully, the parking was free. Keys out of the ignition, I removed the seatbelt which had me bound in route of opening the passenger door for Lauren. Just as I leaned forward to open the driver door, I was brushed with a firm hand, forcing me back into my seat.

Unwilling to loosen the grip which her arm had against my chest, I was forced to remain still, under the direction of Lauren who had not yet explained the meaning of her abrupt nature. Slithering down my seat like a snake, I attempted to escape the bondage which proved unsuccessful. Irritated, I asked, "What now Lauren?" I could see the wetness of her tongue trigger moisture around her lips. Mouthing phrases which only she knew the words, her vocals mute, I couldn't image what was going on through her head.

"We need to talk," she whispered.

Between the near-death experience and Lauren coming on to me every chance she could get, I started to believe this whole evening was a bad idea. The restaurant in plain view, the aroma of the food seeping through all entrances of my car and I couldn't get over how hungry I was, forcing me to rethink my thoughts on calling it a night.

"You want to talk now," I asked, my stomach roaring.

"Yes," she responded with a soft cry.

This conversation had better be worth every pound I was shedding, growing hungrier by the second. If Lauren was about to play games tonight, we could cut this evening short and return home as I'd made it clear where I stood. Interrupted numerous times by the sound of my phone, Lauren took it upon herself to claim ownership of my handheld device, turning it off completely. Placing my phone into the glove box where it no longer existed to the human eye, she attempted, for the second time, to speak whatever was on her mind.

"I should have said this a long time ago," she shook her head.

On her chest, she placed her hand, completely humble with her words. For the first time in a long time, I was reunited with Mackenzie, the familiar stranger I now knew to be Lauren whom I once loved so much. Speaking with great emotion, "From the bottom of my heart Chris, I appreciate you. I cannot think of any man who would do all that you have done for me and my son."

Fighting past the tears, "The way that I left things that day after church, I know that I hurt you." Appetite diminished, I leaned in, sitting at the edge of my seat, using my steering wheel as a crutch. In my heart, I believed I was getting ready to hear an apology. This apology would serve as much closure and lead us into the right direction of co-parenting.

This apology would confirm that I did in fact do all that I could as a man for Lauren and that the direction which our past relationship went, was not a reflection on me. Meeting me halfway, Lauren also leaned in, placing her hand on mine. Lost in the message I believed she was driving home, I allowed her hand to remain on top of mine. Our eyes interlocked, she continued, "You are to blame for absolutely nothing." And here it was.

"Chris, I am..............."

Her words cut short, the two of us distracted by the bright light that appeared to be aiming our way. This car, coming so fast, we could hear the tires losing tread as the rubber melted into the concrete. No time to run for cover, I reached over with my entire body, shielding both Lauren and my unborn son. In the blink of an eye, the car was hit.

Clouds of smoke circulating all around, a bright light reflecting from what was left of my rear-view mirror, and all that remained on my mind; were we still alive? Frantic, I removed my hands, which covered both Lauren and my son. Frightened, her breaths short, Lauren appeared to still have a pulse. Thinking in my head, had this accident been caused a couple of weeks later, my son could have been the innocent victim of a fatality as he would have been in the backseat where the base to his car seat had recently been installed.

Aiding Lauren as she slowly lifted from a fetal position near the dashboard, I began wiping off debris caused by the other car which rested in my backseat. Visible to the eye, Lauren had sustained some cuts and scrapes from the glass, the back of her neck dressed in a red undertone, drips of blood leaking out.

"What the hell? Lauren are you ok," I frantically asked.

Coughing, the smoke buildup increasing, Lauren patted her body down, pressing against her stomach. Her words slurred as she hit her head on the dashboard, she responded, "I think so."

A reckless coward, the driver of the car that without a doubt, caused this crash, remained idle in his or her seat. It was clear that they were alive from the movements displayed and not once did they rush to our aid. Hard to make out a description, their windows were tinted, the parking lot poorly lit, not to mention the sun had set. Staggering out of the driver side door, I walked around front to free Lauren of a damaged vehicle and to get she and the baby to a safer environment. Into my arms she jumped as I held her hand out of the car. Holding her close, I could feel her body shiver. Her head resting on my chest, my hands holding on to her back, I stood and watched as the driver, who caused the crash, slowly exited the vehicle.

Without a single breath of an apology, this man or woman stood silent, still, disguised in a hoodie which covered any facial feature. Pissed to the max, I had only sworn to keep my cool to Lauren. This piece of shit here, was about to get all that they had coming to them. Placing my palm onto Lauren's ear as I began to shout from across the way, "What the fuck were you thinking? You could have killed our son."

With every step this person took, I could hear shards of glass catching the soles of his or her feet as they scratched against the ground. Returning the same passion of anger I had given, a familiar voice which I could not quite make out spoke, "What do you mean your muthafuckin child?"

Ruling out the possibility that the voice which I heard before was a female, the more this man spoke, the more familiar his voice became. Parallel to myself and Lauren, the man began to pull back his hoodie. A face once distorted, now plain in sight. No longer was there a question of identity, this person I was well acquainted.

This same car which remained trapped in my backseat was the exact car that trailed us five miles, almost killing us as we shared the road. The sound of the tires as he increased speed just before hitting us was of the same sound I recall hearing as I remained lifeless on the church grounds. This person, who stood and watched as I held Lauren in my arms was none other than, Marcus Banks, Lauren's husband. You could smell the scent of alcohol which covered his entire body, the light just above Marcus highlighting his eyes, red, glossy, filled with venom. Taking two steps forward, I repositioned Lauren, her stomach visible. My palm on her womb, I responded, "This child right here, my son who you almost killed."

Incapable of holding a man to man conversation, Marcus resorted to speaking with Lauren.

With each word he tried to enunciate, his alcohol consumption forcing a slur instead, he began to cry, "I've been looking everywhere for you woman. Here I was thinking this entire time, you'd gone to be with your mother who you said was dying. Please don't tell me this muthafucka has held you hostage this whole time."

Lauren, taking several steps back as Marcus began traveling down memory lane. "You stood in our kitchen that we built together and showed me our baby's ultrasound. We were going to start over as a family of three just like you said." Reverting the conversation back to me, his eyes focused in on Lauren, "What has this man done to you baby?"

I truly understood the misunderstanding Marcus was forced to witness, Lauren held inside my arms considering our past which he had learned. The consumption of alcohol making the situation even worse, there was no reasoning with this man. What he needed to ask was what had his wife done, again? Had Lauren also told Marcus that he was the father of the child she was carrying that she confirmed was mine? Confused again, I scratched my head and asked, in need of understanding, "Hold on here. Lauren, you told me that there was no way Marcus could be the father of this child."

Recalling more dialogue of this significant day which changed my life furthermore, I began to yell, my cool, unkept,

"In fact, you said that he was away on business when you and I conceived this baby. Am I wrong or not?"

Marcus, unable to hold and keep his balance, pointed his finger, hostility on a thousand, "Look bitch, how many times do I have to tell you to stay away from my wife?"

Walking towards him, I wanted desperately to explain to Marcus that this picture he stumbled upon was anything, but an affair he had his mind made to believe, "Listen to me Marcus. This is not even close to what you think it is bro."

Jabbing his fists in the air, attempting to mirror the altercation we had on church grounds, I was not caught off guard today. I had the upper hand this time around, but had no desire to inflict pain on a man who had already experienced so much. All I wanted was to tell Marcus what my position was and walk away from this mess caused by the most deceitful woman who was still up to no good even under my nose. Declining to hit him several times, Marcus had a one-track mind, listening to not a single word I had to say.

Falling to the ground twice, Marcus showed no signs of giving up and was determined to see to it that he hit me. His breaths short, "You fucked with the wrong one. Lauren, I called your mother and she told me that she has not seen you in months and that her health couldn't be better. Where the fuck have you been?" Funny for Marcus to mention Laurens mother. On several occasions, including the day I proposed, Lauren cried on my shoulder, heartbroken that she did not have a relationship with her estranged mother. From the sound, this was yet another lie she chose to tell. My hands molded into fists, I wanted to knock the hell out of Lauren.

My morals hard to hold on to, this woman was close to getting a two piece to the face. Her saving grace, the baby in her stomach which I no longer knew if he was mine or her husbands. Standing up for myself as only I could, I was no longer going to live in the shadow of the bad guy because I wasn't. I was a man doing the right thing by a woman who sought nothing more than to make my life hell. If Marcus wanted to know where Lauren had been resting her head since she wasn't going to come clean, I was about to shed some light, or as women say, "Spill the piping hot tea."

I wanted this exposure to bring closure for Marcus because it didn't take a rocket scientist to see that he too, could do better. This woman stood before God and vowed to love, honor, and obey. As upset as I was, he had to be broken.

"Your wife showed up on my door step six months ago claiming to be pregnant by me," I confessed.

Before I could say another word, I was disrespectfully interrupted, "Shut yo lyin ass up. It's thirsty men like you that make it hard for men like me."

If this man would listen, he would know that I was far from thirsty. I had no desire to be with his cheater of a wife. With each and every pass she made, I declined. I just wanted to be a father to my son which I no longer knew if I even had. Reaching for his shoulder, I asked, "Marcus will you please hear me out?"

Shrugging away, Marcus made it impossible to get close. "Fuck you."

His knees pounded into the ground, arms outstretched, Marcus began to plead before Lauren, "I am your husband and I have done everything for you. You are the only woman that I have ever been with. I gave up the NFL for you baby. Has he really been with you this whole time?" Stepping in the way of this heart to heart moment, I did not like the picture Marcus was painting of Lauren's time away. Yes she was with me the whole time, but not the way he was thinking.

In surrender mode, I held my palms up, "Marcus, it's not what you think, but you have to listen."

Wiping his eyes, Marcus returned to his feet. Delivering a look I'd never seen anyone display before, he turned his back and walked away. Left alone with Lauren, standing idle in a dark parking lot and still, she had no words to express to either us. She had allowed all of this to happen and showed no signs of remorse. Her husband preparing to leave, having been so distraught that he would almost kill himself crashing into another car, and not once did she run after him. Not once did she think of anyone else's hurt or how their lives would be affected as she played her charade of a game. I wanted no further dealings with this woman, but before I turned my back for good, I was going to be the voice for all past and future men she stood to harm.

My arms crossed, pacing back and forth in front of her, I questioned, "Don't you think this has gone on long enough? Haven't you caused enough hurt?" Ironically, the light post Lauren stood under just so happened to be on a timer. The parking lot seemed brighter, a light displayed just above Lauren, putting her in the hot seat. No longer did she have anywhere to run, a place to hide. She could only proceed forward, forced to take ownership of her actions.

My shout, attracting guests from the restaurant, "ARE YOU HAPPY WITH YOURSELF? THAT MAN LOVES YOU." Pounding into my chest, "I LOVED YOU. THIS SHIT HAS TO END OR YOU WILL DESTROY LIVES."

Not a single word did she express, instead she released a scream. This scream so loud that it made the glass on the ground tremble. Her actions getting to her, my words sinking in, she placed her fingers onto her temples where she shouted, "I cannot take it anymore. Listen Marcus, Chris." Drowning out her words, I could hear footsteps off to the side of my right ear, picking up speed. A loud click, almost like a pop can just behind my head. My shoulders slowly turned, I looked over to find that I was face to face with the barrel of a gun. My heart pounding out of my chest, I began to breath heavy. My eyes closed, I prayed and asked God that if it was my time that he would forgive all of my sins. Ready to meet my fate, I felt the most forceful shove knock me to the ground, a loud scream from the voice of a female, and POP POP.

"SOMEONE CALL 911."

CHAPTER TWENTY ONE

More Than I Can Bear

I ran behind hospital personnel as they removed Lauren from the ambulance, rushing her into immediate surgery. Held back by one of the RN's, I pleaded entry into the room where it was not only Lauren being seen, but my son. My son, an innocent soul trapped in the womb of his mother. Pushing with all my might, the RN begged, "Sir you have to let us do our jobs. I promise you, we will do all that we can, but I need your patience."

"Please save them. My baby is in there," I cried out.

Watching from the window as they began to cut her clothes, nearing her stomach and I could do no more than pray. The curtains pulled, a sight I could no longer see, I knew in my heart that it was bad. Rocking back and forth in the waiting room, covered in Lauren's blood, I applied pressure to her wound which just wouldn't stop bleeding through even as the EMT's arrived.

"Christopher Harris? Detective Mack. Can you tell me what happened this evening?" My hands held to my face, legs shaking, it all happened so fast. Off to the distance I looked, swaying back and forth, crying out, "He shot her right in front of me."

"Who shot her sir," the detective sat and asked.

Canvassing the few faces that sat in the same waiting room as I, Marcus nowhere in sight, I confessed, "Her husband shot her." Addressing the circumstances surrounding what led to the shooting, my time with the detective had ended. With the information I gave, evidence collected at the scene, Lauren and our child clinging on for dear life, an APB was broadcasted for Marcus Banks who was now a suspect on the run.

Hunched over in a corner, away from the public, I had no one here to help ease the pain or worry that consumed me. The only person I could think to have by my side at this time was Justine and although I did not want to involve her in my personal life, I couldn't face this outcome alone.

Before I even asked, the pain heard in my voice, Justine was in route to the hospital. In my head I could hear my mother say, "Even a man cannot walk through life on his own; at some point you need someone." This made me think a lot of my father. I needed my dad to tell me what to do because I just didn't know. Considering how we left things, our relationship was in no position to add any further complications at this time. The mother of my child was bleeding to death and there was nothing I could do, but wait. Knowing that my child was breathing solely because of Lauren brought me to the heart wrenching reality that if she died, so too could my son. This was all too much for one man to handle.

Justine had arrived the moment I placed a call to my mother. Holding my hand over the speaker of the phone, I whispered to Justine, "Give me a second."

Quiet she remained, Justine not yet aware of all that had happened, she began to pat away at my body, in search of the route of the blood. Reaching for her hand that had made its way up my neck, I placed a soft kiss to her inner fingers, signaling that I was not hurt.

Hysterical, as if she knew what had just occurred, my mother shouted, "Chris, where have you been all day? I've called you over and over again. Why didn't you answer the phone baby?" Now was not the time to deal with her overbearing behavior. With Marcus on the loose, considered armed and dangerous, Lauren barely alive, my son depending on his mother for survival, and my life heading in an unknown direction, I had to place this call on the backburner. Only after hearing back from the doctors would I tell my mother and father what was going on.

"Mom. I can't do this right now. Can we talk later," I asked. Hoping she would end the call quietly, she instead began to cry. "Chris. This cannot wait son." The last time I heard my mother this emotional was when she told me my best friend passed. Unable to take any further bad news, I asked carefully, "Mom why are you crying? What's wrong?"

"Chris, your dad had a heart attack this morning."

Falling backwards, my shoulders hitting the wall, I asked, "But he is ok, right?" My father's heart attack is what saved my life the night Mike was murdered. As he had pulled through the first time, I was praying he would pull through again. I planned to be right by his side, bringing us back to the father and son we were before such an immature argument. My dad was a warrior and I knew he could stand this test.

Asking again, "Mom, is dad ok?" Breathing heavy, "He was on life support all afternoon. Baby I kept trying to call you." Leaning on a prayer for Lauren, my son, and now my father.

Stretched thin, I had made up in my mind that I would stay the night by Lauren's side, making sure both she and my son were in the clear. My father, I would head out tomorrow and be the son he needed me to be, forgetting all of the foolishness. Sending my mother a message to give to my father in my absence, "Tell dad I'll be out first thing in the morning. What's his room number?"

Strange thing, the temperature in the waiting room became extremely cold, no longer anyone in sight, but myself and Justine. The dialogue my mother and I had gone back and forth, stood silent. The only noise I could hear, the electrical circuits of the ceiling lights in the hospital waiting room.

A whistle of air released on the other end of the phone, my mother cried out and informed, "Chris, dad is gone baby. He died an hour ago."

No idea the content of this phone call, Justine stood, holding me, her assumptions made based on my facial expression. Numb to all of the hurt, the pain, the shock, the regret, I had no tears left to cry out. All I had was a lifeless body, withering away, worn out and defeated.

A bright light followed the doctor as he entered in the waiting room also covered in blood. Without any expression on his face, he held a chart in his hand, cleared his throat and asked, "Are you the family of Lauren Banks?"

CHAPTER TWENTY-TWO

One Last Cry

The soft keys played by the pianist, the alignment of flowers displayed perfectly alongside the front of the sanctuary, friends and family members making their way towards the casket and into their seats, it was each vivid image that made this day a sad reality.

My mother, keeping busy as only she could during a time of mourning, made sure everything was in order. From the flowers out in the foyer, the distribution of obituaries, the arrival of the catering service as we returned from the cemetery, even the stance of the ushers as they directed the crowd, my mother made certain there wasn't a single flaw. An unclear mind the last few days, I was doing my best to keep it together for my mother who had her own internal pain to battle. The strong force of comfort for one another, neither one of us yet to fully begin the grieving process.

Directed by the ushers, my mother and I were escorted to our seats as the doors of the church closed shut.

I almost forgot how painful it was to say goodbye to a loved one. As strong as you wanted to be, the outside forces had a way of unintentionally hindering the healing process. If people weren't in and out extending apologies, they were asking how you were doing as if you had an answer, whether or not you'd eaten as if you had any form of an appetite, inquiring how your loved one passed as if it were any of their business, all while you, yourself were trying to make sense of it all. Filled with much regret, I could not help, but wonder what the outcome would have been had I not gone to New York. Had I not been so hell bent and on a quest for this rightful passage of manhood, would life have been any different? Service moving along as planned, the time had come for me to head to the pulpit, introducing myself, speaking to many for the first time. Sister Amani, following the order of service located off of the obituary, prepared the room as I stood weak at the knees, "And now we will have a word from Brother Harris."

Looking down at my greatest accomplishment, my biggest motivation, I placed my eyes on my son, the only form of light in such a world of darkness.

"Would you hold him for me," I quietly asked my mother.

God certainly knew what he was doing bringing C.J. into our lives when he did. Although the pain was very much fresh, C.J. certainly made the days a bit brighter. The picture of health despite all that he had been through, he gave my mother and myself the comfort we needed to push through. After placing a blanket over C.J., the air in the room slightly cool, I walked towards the alter, just before the pulpit, and excused myself in a personal moment of prayer.

My words, in need of direction, I bowed down and prayed, asking God to lead and guide my thoughts. I wanted to touch those in the room who were confused and full of questions, myself included. I knew that only God could make sense of this new-found life and through me, I hoped that he could deliver the very peace we all needed.

"Hallelujah. Thank you, Father," friends and family began to praise. While down on my knees, I felt at ease, God's presence near. Standing tall, feeling refreshed, I carried up the steps, a new-found joy in my soul. The worry and doubt, unanswered questions that I entered into the sanctuary with, were no longer a thought as I looked out into the crowd.

Adjusting the microphone that sat on top of the podium, I paused for a brief moment, interrupted by a tiny voice in my head that whispered, "You've got this Chris."

The words of encouragement from an angel above, stood all the support I needed to push forward in my speech. No longer in need of the tiny notecard I had allowed my nerves to dismantle, I tucked it back inside of my pants pocket and allowed God to use my tongue as he saw fit.

"Good morning church," I greeted.

In unison, everyone responded, "Good morning."

"For those who do not know me, my name is Christopher Harris. On behalf of the entire family, we say thank you for your letters, cards, thoughts, encouraging words, and certainly your prayers as they are needed at this time." Blank stares at first, I took a step back and asked God to show himself in this place.

Not even ten seconds and my prayer had been answered.

The spirit began to move in me and into my hand, I took the microphone, removing it from its stand.

Ordering my steps, I began to walk off the pulpit and down the center aisle.

"I walked into this very sanctuary this morning filled with doubt, asking why Lord why? Why take a loved one away from a host of people that need them here on earth? Why allow so much hurt to arise? I stand in front of each of you today to let you know, these are not questions for us to know the answer," I confirmed. Pointing my finger up to the sky, "He has a plan for our lives and once we have completed our mission here on earth, he calls us back home. Our loved ones are simply temporary figures for us to borrow until their purpose is complete."

"I find comfort knowing that the person we have all

grown to love, is now resting in the arms of the Lord. There is no more hurt, no more pain, and no more sorrow. We each hold on to special memories we don't want to let go."

Removing the microphone far from my lips, I paused for a brief moment, my focus no longer on those gathered. A part of me felt that I was misleading the crowd as the memories locked inside my head were far different from the ones I'm certain they held close. The memories I recalled were ones I desperately wanted to rid my thoughts of entirely.

Distracted briefly, it was the sound of the sweetest infant cry from C.J. that reaffirmed God's presence in this place. Here I was, focused on a past that had me bound for so long and while I thought I had not one positive memory to lean on, I had one far better than any other memory in the room. My son, C.J., outweighed each and every bad day, bringing my focus back to a peaceful state. With a smile on my face, looking at the creation held in my mother's hands, I touched in the most vague way possible, "I'm forever grateful to have been blessed with a beautiful son which Lauren and I conceived out of love."

"To many, the journey of she and I is one of confusion and mystery for myself included."

I could have said a lot more, illustrating my time with Lauren, but I was not going to tarnish her name just to prove that I was not at fault for wrecking a marriage or even her death. This was the homegoing celebration for my son's mother and we were going to respectfully send her off the best we could. Holding the microphone down again, I leaned in to place a kiss on my son's tiny forehead, amazed at how much he looked like his mother. More her than me to be exact and it was comforting knowing that each time he looked into the mirror, he would be able to see her face.

"Our son will always be reminded of his mother and the sacrifice that she made just for him. While in the hospital, Lauren was forced to make a decision to have an emergency Csection which could cause further bleeding or wait it out, our son having only a 30% chance of survival. Deciding to save our son and not herself, the doctors informed that she was alive long enough to witness our sons birth. Into the gates of heaven, she was able to take an image of our child which she'll always have," I began to cry.

Fighting back the tears, I concluded, "I am rejoicing at her bravery which has allowed my son to be here today. I ask that you all continue to keep Lauren's mother, father, husband, and our son in prayer as we each find the strength to press forward." What started as an applause by my mother alone, many still processing in their minds what they believed to be, a love affair turned deadly, transitioned into a standing ovation. Appreciative of the gesture, I had not stood before the room to gain recognition or even prove that I was an innocent victim in a love triangle. From this, I wanted to shed my last cry and say goodbye.

Greeted by Pastor as he entered and I exited the pulpit, he whispered comforting words into my ear, where I was the only one who could hear. He knew much more than I had allowed the crowd to know and praised my humbleness. If it had not been for my mother, Justine, also out in the crowd, and C.J, I'm not certain I would have made it to this day. Requesting that I meet him in his office once service ended, I asked Justine to assist my mother with C.J. which she agreed without hesitation. Side by side they took to the center aisle, C.J. with my mother, Justine carrying the diaper bag.

Passing by the very pew I first laid eyes on Lauren, I took my first step forward, in essence, closing a chapter in my life that brought many life lessons. Shedding my final tears, I walked down the hallway towards Pastors office which remained closed.

Composing myself as I awaited a response to my knock, the door opened slow and in front of me stood a man I had never seen before. Entering into the room with caution, I was afraid that I had just interrupted a counseling session as Pastor sat at a table with an unknown woman, the unknown male returning to an out of place chair.

Distance kept, Pastor motioned for me to join, sitting in the fourth and final vacant chair. This chair, tucked under the very table three others occupied of which I only knew one. Not sure what Pastor had up his sleeve or what assistance I could offer, I followed the command and pressed forward.

My palms pressed firmly onto the table as I made my way into the chair, I watched in front of me, Pastor offer tissue to a crying woman I had yet to be introduced. Eyes front, fingers interlocked, Pastor introduced, "Chris, this is Mr. Thomas and Miss. Smith. Do you notice any resemblance?"

Was this a trick question? Zooming in, eye balls extended out of each socket, I glanced over at my left then over to my right, not a single recollection of memory.

"I cannot say that I do sir," I shrugged.

Taking the lead in conversation, the gentleman formally introduced himself, his hand outstretched, "Hello Chris, my name is Mr. Thomas. This here is Miss. Smith. We are Lauren's parents." As long as I wanted to meet Lauren's parents, never had I imagined it to be under such circumstances.

Correcting my somewhat slouched position, offering the utmost respect, I humbly expressed, "Ma'am, Sir; I am truly sorry for your loss." Placing her hand onto my shoulder, Lauren's mother responded, "Honey, we are the ones who are sorry." Lauren and her mother had very similar physical appearances. Their tone of voice almost a complete match, but the apology; however, although appreciated, was far from the same. This apology, one Lauren's mother felt compelled to offer, came from the wrong mouth and honestly; I no longer dwelled on hearing it. Keeping my comments to myself, I listened as she had more to say.

"We know that our daughter was no saint, but I assure you, she was brought up better than she displayed. Lauren's father and I have spent much time resenting one another because of her. After twenty-six years of marriage, she placed a wedge so far between us, we stood no chance of repair and felt it best to divorce. The hardest thing a mother could do is walk away from her child, but she left me no alternative, her road to destruction fast and fierce."

"Just maybe if I stayed around, she would have turned out different," Lauren's mother said, reaching for tissue. "I am truly sorry to both you and my son in-law Marcus for all of the pain that has been done to you."

If only her parents really knew, I thought to myself. Twiddling my thumbs, biting down on my bottom lip, I questioned whether or not to bring Lauren's mother and father into my world over the course of nine months. Thinking like a man who sought to move on, I found this disclosure to be irrelevant. Out of respect for the deceased and to also block further pain in which her parents would be forced to endure, I left the past in the past.

Left alone, I became excluded from a secretive conversation both Lauren's mother and father began to whisper, occasionally glancing over in my direction. Wanting not to be rude, I waited for their dialogue to cease as I prepared to leave, returning to Justine, my mother, and my newborn son. The whispers lasting more than ten minutes, obvious that I was no longer needed, I stood from my chair, pushed it under the table, and asked, "Will there be anything else Pastor?"

"No son, I do believe that is all unless the two of you have anything else," he asked. Nudging one another as if they were brother and sister bickering, I could hear words muffled, but not clear enough to decipher from the direction of Lauren's mother. Aiding or should I say, speeding up the conclusion of this meeting, I asked, "Did you say something Miss. Smith?"

Slapping the side of Mr. Thomas's arm, Lauren's mother sat close to the edge of her seat, playing around with her fingers. Rubbing her hands in a circular motion around her knees, she breathed in and out. With much hesitation, she asked softly, "We were just wondering, if it is at all possible, and please feel free to say no, but we were just wondering if we could meet our grandson? I just want to see his face, that's all." Not one to ever deny my son an opportunity to bond with his mother's side of the family, I did not have to think twice about answering such a beautiful request. My heart filled with joy knowing C.J. would have constant reminders of his mother surrounding him, I escorted his grandparents out to the car where my mother stood.

"Follow me," I allowed my hand to direct our path.

I hoped, for the sake of my son, that they would remain in C.J.'s life. At some point, C.J. would have lots of questions about his mother's past and there was only so much that I could address. Mr. Thomas and Miss. Smith, having birthed Lauren, could fill in the gaps for him.

I knew that it was going to take a village to raise my son especially if we wanted to keep Lauren's memory alive. Exchanging contact information, but not before Miss. Smith brought C.J. to her chest where she placed a tiny kiss to the top of his head and embraced him as any loving grandparent would. Handing him back over to my mother, she waved, "Nana loves you C.J." Each of us gathered around the baby, I believed this to be a wonderful coping mechanism. Lauren's parents were able to see good come from their daughter's short time here on earth.

Despite the past we had lived, filled with unpleasant memories, Lauren ended this earth, leaving us with a positive future and that future was C.J. How could one remain mad at her for birthing such a blessing? The focus no longer on sadness or hurt, but on our tiny little blessing.

Life certainly had its way of shifting things around. The time off that I spent getting to know my son, my son also got to know me as his father. As young as he was, I never wanted there to be a doubt that I did not love or care for my son. He had all of me and without him, I was nothing. As a single parent, I could not lie, it was hard to balance fatherhood along with the demands of my job which Justine was lenient of my situation. Thank goodness for my mother, who had moved in temporarily to help. Coming home each day without dad was proving very hard for her which is why I believed she jumped at the opportunity to travel here to New York.

Not sure what I would do without the women in my life, I was blessed to have my mother right by my side to take care of the baby while I worked. I appreciated Justine working around my schedule so that I had ample time in the morning to bond with C.J. and also return home at a decent hour. Even Lauren's mother, I was thankful for. Although she did not live close to New York, she was sending clothing and other infant essentials faithfully, not one item I was unable to use or that he would not grow into.

We were making it through, minute by minute, day by day. My faith tested, now stronger than ever, there was one final piece to the entire ordeal with Lauren; Marcus's court date which I was called as the star witness. As much as I did not want to be a part of a trial that stood to reopen many doors I believed I already closed, I had to remind myself; after this final roadblock, it was all over. Just C.J. and I to live a positive life of father and son.

CHAPTER TWENTY THREE

Verdict

The district attorney's office had built a case against Marcus for the murder of Lauren. Subpoenaed by the court, I had no choice, but to stand before a jury and testify.

Marcus, escorted by two officers as he entered into the courtroom, kept his face out of sight as the reporters aligned the room. On his body he wore an orange jumpsuit, handcuffs which had his wrists bound, and shackles which kept his legs from walking a clear path, one he'd battled to stay on for some time now. His appearance, on display for the general public, you couldn't help, but feel for him. No longer called by his government name, his new identity that of a set of numbers, engraved in the material of his chest pocket. A face covered with facial hair as though he had not shaved since that night and one could hardly recognize him.

A stare over into my direction as I sat behind him on the prosecution side and instantly, his head lowered onto the table which he and his attorney shared. Impossible to keep my eyes off of him, a part of me still wanted to share all that I had attempted, never imagining that we would be here today. I wanted to desperately address to the courts that although his actions were inexcusable, they were not the actions of a loving husband who had the world in his hands, but a broken man, triggered by love, deceit, and pain within. This man had taken all that he could until he just snapped.

Three months alone in a cold jail cell, I had no doubt in my mind that Marcus had spent enough time secluded from the world to regret his actions which took a life and not just any life, his wife's and the mother of my child.

Facing twelve years behind bars, I hoped that the testimony I gave, would not incriminate him further, but assist the judge to issue a more lenient sentence. Answering question after question from both the prosecuting and defense team, my words were documented by each attorney, recorded, Marcus's fate hanging in the wind.

In my head, I replayed that night over and over again, wishing Marcus would have only listened. I tried desperately to tell him that I was not messing around with his wife, but he wouldn't listen. I tried to tell him about our first date, how Lauren told me that she was single which I asked before going any further, but he wouldn't listen. I tried to tell him that she came knocking on my door, claiming that I was the father of her unborn child, but he wouldn't listen. I tried to tell him that when questioning who in fact was the father of the baby she was carrying, she denied any dealings with him, leaving myself the only other potential candidate, but he wouldn't listen. I tried to tell him that what he saw that night, was nothing more than a father's love and protection for his child which is where my hostility spiraled, but he wouldn't listen. I wanted desperately to express that like him, I was hurt too, but he just would not listen.

I had seen my share of courtrooms thanks to Mike going in and out of juvenile with his hot temper and rebellious ways, but never had I sat before the court and testified against anyone. To someone like Keenan, my appearance on the stand could be misconstrued as "snitching," but in fact, my goal was to do the opposite. From my testimony, I wanted to help Marcus. In a position where he was finally forced to hear me out, I began the retelling of a blank canvas, turned masterpiece, ruined by disaster. The beginning, middle, and tragic end I uncovered, aiming each and every vivid detail towards the center of Marcus's eardrums.

Bonded by the love we both shared for the woman Marcus knew to be Lauren, I knew to be Mackenzie, we had both lost our way and for that realization, I stood proud to defend Marcus. Even if my words had no impact on the jury, I wanted him to know that I supported him completely.

Caught in the moment of insecurity, believing he stood a chance of losing his wife, instead of confronting Lauren on the issues at hand, he directed his anger instead, on the other man; myself. This here act, a societal problem which proved detrimental.

Looking back, I understood how both encounters Marcus stumbled upon painted a picture of Lauren and I together, but in the grand scheme of things, she was never mine nor his. Lauren stood for herself alone. She did not care about either of us, but that she obtained all that she wanted, no matter the cost. Even in her passing, Marcus and I were reunited yet again to relive a chaotic past, filled with much regret. Not sure when the time would come as I did not want to think that far ahead, but one day I would have to sit my son down and explain how lies and deceit brought his mother's life to an end. How much I'd disclose, a bridge we'd cross come time.

This new life of mine, I would have to learn how to balance being a stern father and one my son would feel comfortable coming to for anything. In the absence of his mother, I planned to nurture him as best I could so that when the time came for him to feel any form of void, it would be a mild feeling which together, we would cope.

For Marcus, the suffering would not end any time soon. There was no rewind button; the damage, already done. Left for Marcus, a total of two options; a stop button, allowing his sentence to define the brokenness inside or option two, a play button. This button where day by day, he would learn to walk a new path, his head held high, sharing his story to those dealing with similar circumstances. Silence in the courtroom, the only visible sound, that of the judge removing a piece of paper from a manila folder.

"Mr. Banks, if you would stand," the judge asked.

Struggling to stand, Marcus wobbled out of his seat and focused his attention on the judge, his sentence moments from being read.

Holding on to the piece of paper, the judge spoke, "Now in exchange for your testimony, you have asked the court for a DNA test on one infant Christopher Harris, Jr. Is this correct?"

"Yes sir," Marcus responded.

Holding the paper up, the contents which only the judge could see, Marcus was granted one final ray of hope, in effort to help his case.

"The court will submit into evidence, the DNA test results which I hold in my hand. Before reading, Mr. Banks you may turn to the court and deliver what it is you feel the need," the judge allowed.

Even the blind could see how fast his heart was beating. His eyes, blood shot red, I'm not sure if or when Marcus had a decent night's sleep. The courtroom filled with twelve jurors, a judge, reporters as this case reached the news, both Marcus's and Lauren's parents who sat, hand in hand on the defense side, supporting one another. His eyes closed briefly, Marcus returned to the courtroom, prepared to speak. "I met Lauren when we were fourteen. She was the beautiful cheerleader on the sidelines every guy wanted on their arm. I was the star football player who had to have her.

If you saw her, I was near and if you saw me, she was right by my side. The year I was entered into the NFL draft, Lauren got pregnant and asked me to stay behind which took no convincing.

My love for her and our unborn meant so much more to me than the fame and love for football. After three months carrying our child, we suffered a great loss. The day that Lauren miscarried, I truly believe that day brought a world of indiscretions which at first I tolerated, assuming that in time, her pain would heal and our distant relationship would spark the magic we once shared. I tried so very hard to make her feel whole again, but a void remained visible, one I just could not fill. Fearing that I was losing her, I did what any man would do to prove his undying love.

I got down on one knee and asked her to be my wife." Taking a moment to catch his breath, Marcus continued. "Dreams of becoming a football player no longer a possibility, I hoped that my drive and determination to become a fire fighter would bring her joy and excitement. As much as I prayed and hoped she would admire my career, it was my distance with a demanding job that forced her to slip away, no one's fault, but my own. There were many nights when I would rush home, prepare dinner, dim the lights, set the music, bring home flowers and through the front door, she wouldn't enter. I began following my wife when a close friend claimed to have spotted her with another man and with my own eyes after much research, it was confirmed that in fact she was in the arms of another man. A million thoughts running through my head and all I saw was red. In my eyes, Chris was wining and dining my wife, disrespecting myself as her husband and giving her no opportunity to make things right at home."

His facial expression, a mild touch of peace, quickly fell back into anger accompanied by tears. "Things were ok once I found Lauren and brought her back home. Our marriage back on track, the icing on the cake, her confirmed pregnancy. I couldn't wait to be a father and I was so thankful that God granted us a second opportunity at parenthood which I couldn't stop telling the world."

Resting on the table he and his attorney shared, Marcus opened up a door that both the jurors and myself walked through for the very first time.

"The thought of becoming a father was amazing," he

said, his face glowing in that moment. If nothing else, the jurors could tell that Marcus did in fact love his wife very much.

"There for Lauren hand and foot the entire first trimester, I asked nothing of her, but to relax. She didn't have to work or lift a finger. All I wanted was for our son or daughter to enter into this world prepared to receive all the love he or she could stand." Biting down on his lip, Marcus looked out to the distance, his facial expression shifting from a state of bliss to a blank stare.

"A phone call to my wife, the caller never identified, and my wife was on the next flight to visit her mother who did not have much time left. Believing her story, I allowed the public to care for my wife, praying she was in good hands as I was on call the entire week and unable to escort her out of town. Missing her like crazy, I began placing call after call, text after text all forms of communication, without answer. Not a single confirmation that she made it safely to her destination and this is where my worry began. Wanting not to bother her family in their time of bereavement, I reached out, with much hesitation to the home of her mother."

Hitting his knuckles on the table several times, warned by the bailiff to compose himself, Marcus was no longer building his character, but instead, displaying a temperamental man, capable of causing harm.

"The reality I received when asking about my wife, not at all what I expected. Hearing her mother's upbeat voice answer the phone," Marcus pointing out to the crowd, "Was not sick at all, I lost it. I declared a nationwide search, allowing nothing or no one to stand in my way. What little information I had, I used to search every corner of the earth. I started with the church that hosted the picnic my friend claimed to have spotted Lauren. At first I doubted my friends accusations, but the sincerity in this man's voice, a man who only knew how to crack jokes, I believed there to be truth to what he had to say. I walked right into the church, fitting in perfectly. In search of any ministry where the name Chris rang a bell, luck appeared on my side. I learned that he was not only the head of a couple of ministries I pretended to show interest, but that he was well known around town for his dedication to the youth in the community.

This tip, the biggest of all, led me straight to his place of employment. An exact location, I wasn't sure how to approach the situation, if it was a situation at all. Fearing that I could be chasing a dead end, I parked across the street and waited while attempting to talk myself out of this madness. Chris's face engraved in my head, one I would never forget, I cracked my window, my head frozen still, zooming in at the front door of the center. I'd hit the jackpot around 5:30 p.m., Chris exiting out of the building. My adrenaline high, I followed him on the main road, hoping he would lead me to my wife if he was with her at all. Trailing behind for a short while, we stumbled upon a parking garage which required an i.d. Without one, I had to stand down until I figured out my next move.

As the time went by, the sun starting to set, I kept saying to myself, "stay calm, don't yell, and be open to listen."

I did not want a repeat episode such as the one at the church because truth be told, that was not my character at all. It was a temporary moment of insanity, one I vowed to never allow myself to revisit.

After camping out in my car for an hour, I spotted the marked car for a second time. This time it was exiting the garage, leaving me full access to trail behind. I had no idea what I was doing, where I was going, what I would say when the time came or who the passenger was that occupied the front seat, only a silhouette imaging in the side mirror. It wasn't until we turned the corner that the cool breeze from the windows opening, repositioned this woman's bangs which prompted her to look out into the side mirror. Those beautiful eyes, reflecting in the mirror and BOOM, there she was. Chris was parading around town with my wife, disregarding the warning

I had already delivered. Attack mode was the name of my game and Chris was my prey."

Looking directly into my eyes, the remainder of the conversation I believe he wanted me to feel. His finger aimed straight at me, I could feel the dagger going into my chest. "This man had my wife blindsided, her heart held hostage, keeping her from me. This man had been around my child, stealing precious developmental moments that a real father would want to be involved. Enraged, I no longer saw clearly. My mindset so distorted, I entered into a state of shock, my foot wedged on the gas pedal and before I knew it, I crashed into the back of Chris's car."

There wasn't a single body in the courtroom that did not sit on the edge of their seats while Marcus uncovered the events of that night where lives were forever changed. Disregarding the first order to calm down, Marcus pounded his entire fist into the woodgrain table, particles lodged into his knuckles as he began to cry out. The guilt of what he had done a painful reality, Marcus could not contain his emotions. Squinting his eyes now halfway closed, the water just barely holding still in the corners of each eye lid, "I sat in the car for a moment just looking at him console my wife, an act stripped away from me while she was away.

Her body, perfectly fit and positioned into his arms as if this were a position she'd frequented. My mind and actions no longer in my control as I was a man who stood nothing to lose. I don't even remember getting out of the car that night for that part, a complete blur to me. I do recall exchanging words, however. Specifically, an entire sentence Chris had on replay as he said it a total of three times, YOU COULD HAVE HARMED MY CHILD.

Not only had he taken my wife from me, but the opportunity at a second chance to father a child and I wanted him dead. I wanted him out of the picture forever and the only way I knew how was to end his life the way he painfully tried to end mine. I didn't even turn to look when I pulled the trigger. I didn't stay to watch his body drop. I just shot and ran." Multiple gasps of air echoed throughout the room, many in shock at the climax of such a tragic reality.

"I had no idea that my wife had jumped in between us. I spent my whole life trying to protect her from the world," tears spewing down his cheek, "and I was her biggest danger." Overwhelmed with pain, his attorney brought to his feet in an effort to console a broken client who was also the husband to the deceased. Turning back to the judge, he did his best to contain his outburst of an expression, "I loved my wife so much sir. I swear to God I did not mean to hurt her."

His eyes faced forward, Marcus leaned forward onto the table and stated, "Chris, I am sorry man." Shaking his head, breathing through a tiny exit of his lips, "You tried to tell me man. Had I listened and not loved so hard just maybe we wouldn't be here today. Not a day goes by where I don't question my actions that night. This was not supposed to be my life," his arms raised, displaying his handcuffs.

"I couldn't even say goodbye to my wife or attend her funeral. I missed the birth of the baby and for what because my wife found happiness with someone else," he owned.

The chime from the handcuffs colliding together as Marcus positioned his hands in prayer form, pleading with the judge, "Sir, I just need to know if C.J. is my son or not. I need to know if my actions were worth it which I admit were all wrong."

Taking his seat, he sobbed aloud, repeating one final time, "I just need to know sir." Not a dry eye in the room, even the judge who tried hard to keep it bottled inside. Choked up inside, his emotions tugged, the judge accepted Marcus's testimony.

"Thank you, Mr. Banks. The court will now receive the

DNA test into evidence. Will both Marcus Banks and Christopher Harris please stand before the court?"

I felt horrible knowing that no one would be there to pick up further pieces of Marcus's life once he learned what I already knew, C.J. was not his, but my son. The similarities in appearance, the bond we shared, it was undeniable that I was in fact the father and I hoped the results would offer some sort of closure for Marcus.

"In the case of the defendant, Mr. Marcus Banks, the DNA test concludes with a 99.9 percent accuracy, that you are not the father of one Christopher J. Harris, Jr." My hands held tightly on the banister which separated myself and Marcus from one another, I was relieved. As much as I was certain baby C.J. was mine, it was comforting hearing that we could eliminate Marcus.

I could not; however, allow my excitement to show because truth be told, this was not a day to celebrate. There was no trophy either one of us stood to accept after all was said and done.

This was the first day of many new beginnings for us both. Although the new beginning started off rough for Marcus, I knew that he was going to come out of all of this on top.

The judge, clearing his throat, read the final result. This result I could have read aloud myself. Out of respect, I allowed him the floor to confirm to the world, including news reporters, what I already knew.

"In the case of Mr. Christopher Banks, the DNA test concludes with 99.9% accuracy, you are not the father of one Christopher J. Harris, Jr."

ABOUT THE AUTHOR

Jasmine 'Lanae' Herring was born and raised in Indianapolis, Indiana. A wife and mother of three, the new author is on the rise to becoming one of the best, well-written female authors.

A social butterfly, Jasmine utilizes her interpersonal skills to shape and develop suspenseful dramas that readers are sure to relate.

It is simply impossible to open a Jasmine Herring novel and not find yourself on a journey in which you have either traveled in the past or are currently trailing.

When asked what's next for the rising author, her response, simply put, "Endless stories to cure hearts."

Black Butterfly Books

an imprint of

The Butterfly Typeface Publishing.

Books to intelligently entertain the discriminating reader!
Contact us for all your
publishing & writing needs!

Iris M Williams
PO Box 56193
Little Rock AR 72215

www.butterflytypeface.com

www.ingramcontent.com/pod-product-compliance
Lightning Source LLC
Chambersburg PA
CBHW050519260626
47157CB00004B/1384